The Drum, the Doll,
and the Zombie

THE DRUM, THE DOLL, AND THE ZOMBIE

JOHN BELLAIRS
Completed by Brad Strickland

*Frontispiece
by Edward Gorey*

*Dial Books for Young Readers
New York*

Published by Dial Books for Young Readers
A Division of Penguin Books USA Inc.
375 Hudson Street
New York, New York 10014

1 3 5 7 9 10 8 6 4 2

Library of Congress Cataloging in Publication Data
Bellairs, John.
The drum, the doll, and the zombie / John Bellairs
completed by Brad Strickland
frontispiece by Edward Gorey.—1st ed.
p. cm.
Summary: When thirteen-year-old Johnny Dixon and his friend
Professor Childermass try to save the life of the elderly Dr. Coote,
they find themselves facing the forces of a menacing voodoo cult.
ISBN 0-8037-1462-9 (trade).—ISBN 0-8037-1463-7 (lib. bdg.)
[1. Mystery and detective stories. 2. Supernatural—Fiction.]
I. Strickland, Brad. II. Title.
PZ7.B413Dr 1994 [Fic]—dc20 93-43964 CIP AC

Thanks to those who helped:
Gregory Nicoll, Steve Nesheim, Wendy Webb
—B.S.

*For Jeanne Sharp,
one of Johnny's best friends*

B.S.

The Drum, the Doll,
and the Zombie

CHAPTER ONE

"Charley, I'm throwing this shindig for *you*. Now start having a good time, or I'll boot you out into the storm!" grumbled Professor Roderick Childermass. He was a short, elderly man with a nest of white hair, wildly sprouting white muttonchop sideburns, and a pitted red strawberry of a nose. The professor stood before a fireplace in his living room. Sitting on the brick hearth with their backs to the crackling fire were Johnny Dixon and his friend Byron Ferguson, and hunched miserably in an armchair was Dr. Charles Coote, the object of the professor's scorn.

A specialist in the folklore of magic who taught at the University of New Hampshire, Dr. Coote was a tall, reedy man of about seventy, his head crowned with fluffy white hair and his long, bent nose supporting thick, horn-rimmed bifocal glasses. "I'm sorry, Roderick," he muttered. "I'm afraid I haven't exactly been the life of the party tonight."

"The *death* of the party is more like it," snorted Professor Childermass in his abrupt way. "Right, boys?"

Johnny and Byron exchanged glances. Both were about thirteen. Johnny was short and blond, and wore glasses; Byron—who preferred to be called Fergie—was taller and more athletic, with jug ears, curly black hair, a droopy face, big feet, and a devil-may-care attitude. For a moment after the professor's challenge, the two friends just looked at each other. Johnny did not like taking sides in a disagreement between adults, but Fergie grinned and jumped right in. "You said it, Prof," he agreed. "Even before this storm started, the doc was a regular wet blanket."

It was nine o'clock in the evening of a late-September Saturday during the mid-1950s. An equinoctial gale had blown into Duston Heights, Massachusetts, at sunset, and now a dismal wind howled outside as a cold, pelting rain rattled the windows. The nor'easter had brought chilly temperatures, and the professor's first fire of the season was a welcome defense against the cool and the damp.

Dr. Coote sighed deeply. "I am sorry if I'm spoiling everyone's good time," he said. He took a sip from his mug of spiced cider, and his glasses fogged from the vapor. He appeared not to notice. "The truth is, I've been jumpy ever since coming back from New Orleans two weeks ago. Something rather odd happened to me there, and I have yet to figure out what it meant."

Setting his empty mug on the mantel, the professor leaned against the chimney and lit one of his black-and-gold Balkan Sobranie cigarettes. "Well, spill it, Charley. You are among friends here. This storm is too brutal for you to drive back to New Hampshire anyway, and I obviously have to offer you a bed for the night. If I must share my house with you, I simply will not have you moping around like a Gloomy Gus. So you might as well tell us your story."

"Yeah," said Fergie, who had just finished his second slice of the professor's famous German chocolate cake. "Tell us, Doc, what happened 'way down yonder in New Orleans? Ya get chased through the bayous by Albert the Alligator?"

Johnny felt sorry for Dr. Coote, who merely smiled in a mildly pained way at Fergie's little joke. Dr. Coote was a timid soul, not at all like the bombastic Professor Childermass, who terrified practically everyone in Duston Heights with his prickly personality and explosive mannerisms. However, over the past several years Johnny had come to know and like the cranky old man, who had a warm heart beneath his gruff exterior.

Johnny's mother had died some time before. His father, who was a veteran bomber pilot, had rejoined the Air Force to fly fighter planes when the Korean War broke out. Because of that, Johnny had moved from New York

State to Duston Heights, where he lived with his grandparents across from Professor Childermass on Fillmore Street. The Korean War had recently ended, but the Air Force needed Johnny's dad to train pilots for the Strategic Air Command. Since the assignment involved a lot of travel, Major Dixon saw Johnny only a couple of times a year. The rest of the time Johnny spent with his grandparents, or with Fergie, or with Professor Childermass and his few friends.

Dr. Coote coughed self-consciously and finished the last of his hot cider. "I know the story sounds silly," he murmured. "And yet the incident has preyed on my mind in, well, a most unpleasant way. It all began when I traveled to New Orleans to attend the annual meeting of the North American Folklorists' Association. The conference took place from Thursday morning through Sunday noon. You know how these academic conferences are, Roderick—"

"Indeed I do," growled Professor Childermass, his eyes glittering behind his rimless spectacles. "Pack of pompous old fools reading gassy essays to each other and telling one another how smart they are. The worst of it is they think they're all having such a *marvelous, interesting, informative* good time. Phooey on that! Give me a good old Red Sox baseball game any day of the week!"

"Well—I think if you are to understand the story, I had better show you something. It's just outside in my car." Dr. Coote went to the front closet, where he retrieved his comfortably worn camel's-hair topcoat. He bundled into it and clapped on his battered homburg. Then he dashed into the storm. In a moment he was back, holding a brown paper bag that the rain had already soaked. He set it down before the fire and shrugged out of his coat. "Heavens, but the wind is ferocious! Are you boys going to be all right?"

"Uh—sure," answered Johnny, his gaze on the wet paper bag.

"Of course they are," said Professor Childermass. "Byron is spending the night with John. Stop stalling, Charley. What happened at this pretentious academic conference that's got you as spooked as a lone kitty-cat lost in a dog kennel?"

"I was, ah, coming to that," said Dr. Coote. He sank into his chair again, removed his rain-spattered spectacles, and fished a crumpled handkerchief from his side pocket to polish them. "Well, everything went all right until Saturday evening, just two weeks ago tonight. At seven, I took part in a panel discussion about Caribbean folklore research. Somehow or other we got onto the voodoo cults of Haiti and St. Ives, and I am afraid I sounded off a bit. You know, I have done some research preparatory to writing a book on the subject, and—"

"Yes, we know how brilliant you are," interrupted Professor Childermass rudely. "Get to the point! What happened?"

Dr. Coote coughed and replaced his glasses. "Well, at the end of the session, a young man came up to me. He told me he was from the island of St. Ives, and that I had several points exactly right, but that others needed clarifying. 'Above all,' he said, with a frightened look around him, 'you must discover how to deal with the Sect of the Baron. You must learn how to defeat the terrible Priests of the Midnight Blood. You must beware of the walking dead. And whatever you do, you must take this and destroy it if you can!' " With a shudder Dr. Coote picked up his mug, only to discover that it was empty. He took a deep breath. "Then the young fellow handed me the article that is in that paper bag, and he melted away into the crowd. I tried to follow, but he lost me."

Professor Childermass tossed the stub of his cigarette into the fire. "And what was this booby prize? Johnny, you are closest. Open it, if you please."

"Sure, Professor!" Johnny had been itching to know what lay inside the sodden paper bag. He tore away the paper and pulled out a strange little drum that was shaped like a Dixie cup, tapering from top to bottom, although it was larger than a paper cup. The drum was about four inches across at the head and three inches at the bottom. Its head and bottom covering were both of some odd, pebbled leather, the color a deep olive green streaked with yellow and dark-brown stripes. The body of the drum was smooth black wood, carved all in one piece. Red leather thongs tied the drumhead down, running in a zigzag line all around the drum, their ends wound around the ends of small white bones. Other thongs tied to the lower ends of the bones held the bottom covering taut. Between the bones red, green, gray, blue, and white circles had been painted on the body of the drum. Each circle held an emblem: a grinning white skull, a black top hat, a wriggling green snake, a yellow bolt of lightning, and a red drop of blood with a teardrop-shaped white highlight.

"For heaven's sake," said the professor, taking the drum from Johnny and turning it this way and that as he looked at it. "Don't tell me this is what gave you the jitters! Why, you can order one just like this from the Montgomery Ward catalogue. It comes with a feather headdress, your very own bow, and a quiver full of rubber-tipped arrows!"

"Oh, indeed?" asked Dr. Coote with a sickly smile. "Tell me, Roderick, does the Montgomery Ward drum include a set of five phalanges? Because that is exactly what those five little white bones are—human finger and thumb bones!"

Fergie jumped up. "Neat-o!" he said. "Hey, Prof, can I take a gander?" Professor Childermass handed him the drum, and Fergie touched the bones one by one, as if he were counting them. He sank back down on the floor in front of the fireplace. "Look, John baby," he said, "real human fingers!"

Johnny regarded the bones curiously. Now he could see that they tapered to delicately rounded ends. Yes, they could very well be the finger and thumb tips of some unlucky person. However, the news did not excite him as it did Fergie. Instead, it made Johnny's stomach feel queasy.

Professor Childermass was scowling. He hated it when anyone showed him up, and he especially hated to have some choice bit of sarcasm turned against him. With a splutter, he began, "Now see, here, Charley, even if those really are human bones—"

"That they are, Roderick," said Dr. Coote, sounding mildly exasperated. "I had an expert at the university take a good look at them. And don't say they must be fakes or fossils. They are genuine bones, and they come from someone who was killed—or at least who lost his hand—relatively recently, within the last century or so."

The frown deepened on the professor's face. "As I was *about* to say, even if these bones are—ahem!—bona fide, they cannot possibly harm you. I'll admit I've heard of vengeful ghosts returning to haunt people who did them wrong. Still, I have never heard of—of a one-handed ghost out to collect his missing whatchamacallits."

"Phalanges," said Dr. Coote helpfully.

The professor's face got red. "Phalanges! All right, drat all punctilious pedagogues, phalanges! *Whatever* they are, they cannot hurt you, and that is my point. They are simply lifeless bits of bone."

Dr. Coote shrugged. "I am not afraid of dry bones, Roderick. I may be more, ah, cautious than you, but I am not a superstitious fool. No, the symbols painted on the drum disturb me more than the bones do. They are emblems of Baron Samedi, the Lord of the Dead, and of his cult. The cult must be the Sect of the Baron. That much is obvious. Aside from that, I am in the dark. I have never read anything about the Midnight Blood priests. But what really bothers me is that I don't know anything in *voudon* that has to do with this drum, and I should."

"And what in thunder is *voudon?*" asked Professor Childermass.

Dr. Coote leaned forward in his chair, clasping his hands before him. "I must explain that most scholars have never studied the St. Ives branch of voodoo. Many have never even heard of it. St. Ives is a tiny Caribbean island with a population of only a few thousand, all descended from French planters who fled from Haiti during a slave rebellion in 1791. Curiously, the French took with them the superstitions and magical practices of the slaves. Today almost no outsiders visit the island because it is not on the regular tourist routes, and getting there is a real problem. The people are very secretive. Their rulers are *bocors*, or priests, of the local voodoo cult, which they call *voudon*. I spent one summer on the island, just after World War II. Since then I have published the only articles about their particular brand of evil voodoo magic."

"Yes, and you are writing a book about it too," said the professor with a smirk. "Charley, you and I have discussed this before, and you are being inconsistent. As

I recall, your opinion was that voodoo is mostly a religion, no more evil than Unitarianism or Shakerism or any other sect."

Dr. Coote shrugged his thin shoulders. "True, but wicked human nature may corrupt any religion and turn it to evil purposes. Just think of the *jihads*, or holy wars, of Islam. For that matter, think of the poor innocent people your very own Catholic church burned as heretics in the Middle Ages."

"No argument there," agreed the professor. "Although, as you say, such terrible events occur more because of people corrupting the doctrines of the church than because of true religious principles."

"Well, the same is true of voodoo," said Dr. Coote. "Most of it appears harmless. Much of it is simply a survival of African religions, with some borrowings from Catholicism and other creeds. However, the *voudon* cult of St. Ives is a terrible, malevolent corruption of the basic beliefs. I know that magic artifacts have great significance to those who use the supernatural power of *voudon* for evil ends. I also know that the ceremonies of the cult take place to the beat of drums. But blast it, I never heard of this *particular* kind of drum having any special significance. The young man who gave this object to me obviously thought it had some unholy enchantment. He also obviously thought that I could disenchant it. He was mistaken. Hang it all, Roderick, *I* don't know what to do with a drum!"

Professor Childermass nodded solemnly. "Then you

have come to the right person," he said. "Relax, Charley. I know exactly what to do with a drum."

Dr. Coote looked up with hope in his eyes. "I thought you might," he said. "Although it's not in your field, you know quite a lot about sorcery and enchantments. Tell me, Roderick, what do I do with this wretched relic?"

His manner sincere, the professor said, "Well, I'll tell you, Charley. You take your drum and you—beat it!" He threw back his head and laughed uproariously.

"Thanks for nothing," grumbled Dr. Coote, leaning back in his chair with an irritated glare at his friend.

As his laughing fit subsided, the professor coughed and grinned. "Forgive me, Charley. You're just letting some lunatic upset you over nothing. To be quite serious for a moment, if I were you, I'd simply stick the drum in the local museum. Or toss it on the top shelf of a broom closet and then forget it."

"Hey, get a load of me, everybody," said Fergie. "I'm a hepcat." He sat cross-legged, with the drum clenched between his knees. "And now I'll perform my famous solo, entitled 'Who Do Voodoo Like You Do, Dear?' "

"No!" shouted Dr. Coote, but he was too late.

Fergie tapped a rhythm on the drum with his fingertips, a quick *rat-a-tat-tat, rat-a-tat-tat*. At the same time he shook his head and sang in a horrible screechy tenor, "Babaloo! Babaloo!"

Immediately a furious, howling blast of wind shook the house to its foundations. Windows rattled and shingles ripped away with a loud tearing sound. The wind screamed down the chimney, sending a billow of black smoke and bright-orange sparks rolling out of the fireplace. Alarmed, Johnny leaped to his feet. A second later something outside the house exploded, and then the lights went out, plunging everything into gloom.

CHAPTER TWO

As it turned out, the explosion that Johnny heard was an electrical transformer. A big maple tree in Mrs. Kovacs' yard fell against an electric pole down the street from the professor's house, and the impact shorted out the transformer on the pole. When it blew, it knocked out the power to that part of Duston Heights. Of course, Johnny did not learn this immediately. For a few minutes he and the others kept busy stamping and slapping out the burning red embers that the wind had blown into the room.

"Fergie, do you see what you did?" snapped Johnny, really irritated with his friend.

In the ruddy glow of the fire Fergie's face showed astonishment. "*Me?* Dixon, I'm innocent! The storm an'

the wind did this, not some creepy-crawly drumbeat!"
Unlike Johnny, Fergie was not very superstitious, and
he always insisted that practically everything had a sci-
entific explanation.

At last, when they had put out all the sparks, Professor
Childermass lit some candles and a kerosene lamp. The
telephone was dead, so he insisted on shepherding Johnny
and Fergie across the street, where Johnny's grandparents
were relieved to see them. In fact, Grampa Dixon was
just getting into his slicker to come and check on the
boys. Grampa was a gangly, slightly stooped old man
with a wrinkled face and a freckled bald head with just
a few strands of hair draped over it. He carried a lighted
kerosene lamp, which he set down on the kitchen table
as he said, "Thanks for th' delivery service, Rod."

"Think nothing of it, Henry," Professor Childermass
said. "I wouldn't dream of sending them out alone in this
storm."

"It is bad, ain't it?" murmured Gramma Dixon, a
somewhat frail woman who wore her white hair in a neat
bun. She ran a hand through Johnny's hair. "Mercy!
You're soaked through. You an' Fergie just hurry an'
change into your pajamas before you catch your deaths.
I declare, I've never seen it storm this bad in my whole
life."

"I dunno 'bout that," replied Grampa. "How 'bout the
hurricane last year? An' what about—" Johnny and
Fergie went to change as the older folks started remi-
niscing about hurricanes, hailstorms, and *really* bad

downpours. The storm began to let up, and both Johnny and Fergie went to sleep around midnight.

The power company restored the electricity the next morning, and Johnny and Fergie saw Dr. Coote drive away in his old blue Chevrolet. "Wonder if he took the crazy bongo with him," Fergie said.

"I don't know," answered Johnny. "But I hope nothing bad happens because of what you did last night."

Fergie snickered. "Man, oh, man, you should've seen your face when the prof brought in the candles. You were white as a tombstone, and your eyes were round as marbles. John baby, I didn't know my voice was *that* bad!"

Johnny mumbled that there were some things that it was better not to fool around with, but Fergie was no longer paying attention. In the bright light of a cool September Sunday, Johnny had to admit that his fears seemed pretty groundless. Of course, it was one thing to laugh at spooky tales as you got ready for church in the cheerful morning daylight, and another to hear them in the dark of night with a terrible storm raging. At least nothing horrible had happened.

As September ended and October began, Johnny found himself occupied with homework and the World Series and plans for a Halloween party. He soon forgot about the drum and Dr. Coote's odd yarn. Of all Johnny's new concerns, the most pressing was the Halloween party. Two years earlier Johnny had decided that he was too old to go trick-or-treating, so he had remained home and handed out candy to the little kids. Still, Johnny had to admit that he missed the fun of dressing up in some outlandish costume.

That was why he volunteered to help when the teachers at St. Michael's School decided to throw a Halloween party to raise money for some badly needed equipment. The older students would dress up in costumes and run the games that the younger kids would enjoy. To Johnny the party was an ideal opportunity: He could have all the fun of wearing a Halloween costume and none of the embarrassment of having crabby grown-ups peer out at him and mutter, "A little *old* for trick-or-treating, ain'tcha, kiddo?"

He was trying to decide what kind of costume to wear. He sort of saw himself as a scary vampire, with a long black cloak, slicked-back hair, and fangs. However, he had two big disadvantages. First, his hair was blond, and all the vampires he had seen in the movies had black hair. Second, he wore glasses, and something told him that a bespectacled Count Dracula wouldn't scare even a first grader. He practiced going around the house without his glasses, and he could see clearly enough to avoid bumping into the furniture. Unfortunately, he was nearsighted, and that meant that he might have a hard time judging the winners in the dart toss contest he and two other students would be running. Johnny could imagine what might happen if some first-grader threw a wild dart and he could not see it in time to jump out of the way.

His grandmother suggested that he go as a clown, but Johnny wanted a better idea than that. Grampa Dixon thought they could make him up as a tramp, which was what he always recommended. After all, a tramp costume could be scrounged up from just any old clothes that lay around the house, and it wouldn't cost a cent. It wasn't that Johnny's grandfather was stingy, but he was reluctant to spend scarce money on an outfit that, after all, Johnny could use only one night a year.

Johnny and Fergie went to different schools, but when Fergie found out about the Halloween party, he said he wanted to come along. And he intended to come in costume. "Why don't we both go as zombies?" he asked. "You know, the walking dead, like Dr. Coote was talking about. Beware the walking dead, John baby. I can see it now: We come in wearing moldy clothes, like we've been buried for weeks. We'll get some green makeup for our faces and rub dirt in our hair. Best of all, my dad's got a fishing outfit with these artificial rubber worms in it. He won't mind if I swipe a few. They look real, and we could plaster 'em down on our faces and have them dripping out our noses an' ears! Whatcha think of that, big John? Scary?"

"More disgusting than scary," said Johnny, making a face. "I don't know about putting rubber worms up my nose, but maybe the zombie idea could work. At least it would take the same kind of old clothes as Grampa's tramp costume."

"Sure," said Fergie. "And let's read up on zombies to see if we're missing anything that will make the costumes even sharper. I'll bet the prof has a book or two in his library that would help. How about payin' him a visit and seeing if he'll loan you a coupla volumes?"

"Okay," agreed Johnny. "And if the zombie plan doesn't work, maybe we can find something else just as good."

And that was why, one Wednesday night toward the end of October, Johnny went across the street to Professor Childermass' house after supper. The professor had not had a great deal of time to spend with Johnny lately. A flu epidemic had hit Haggstrum College and Professor Childermass had taken over classes for another history teacher, Dr. Duquesne, who was very sick. Teaching a double load kept the professor extremely busy and it made his temper even worse than normal. Fortunately, he seemed immune to the disease. His students told each other that the flu germs were afraid to attack the crabby old man.

Johnny rang the doorbell twice before he heard shuffling footsteps. The door opened, spilling a warm splash of light out into the night. Professor Childermass appeared troubled and subdued. "Oh, it's you, John Michael," he said. "Come on in. I hope *you* haven't come bearing ill tidings."

"Uh, no, Professor. I'm not bearing any tidings at all." Johnny stepped into the professor's house. "Why? Have you had bad news?"

Professor Childermass took a deep breath. "Well, yes, I am afraid so. Charley Coote is in the hospital up in New Hampshire."

"Does he have the flu?" Johnny asked.

The professor shook his head. His expression was grim. "No, it's something worse than that. He—well, he's not exactly in his right mind."

They sat at the professor's kitchen table. The kitchen was in its normal messy state, with dirty pots, pans, and dishes stacked in the sink, though it smelled wonderfully of fresh cake and chocolate—baking was just about the professor's favorite hobby. He served up a slice of yellow cake with chocolate-banana icing and poured Johnny a tall glass of milk. Johnny dug in and told the professor how good it was. His friend nodded absently. "What's the matter with Dr. Coote?" asked Johnny.

The professor sat at the table and drank a cup of coffee. "It's rather odd. A doctor on the staff of Mercy Hospital called me. He says that Charley did not show up for his classes on Monday. So around noon someone at the college drove over to his house to check on him. He found poor Charley ill in bed, babbling nonsense. They bundled him off to the hospital, where he kept mentioning my name and phone number over and over again. Except for that he has been making no sense at all, they say. He jabbers about dead people and midnight and that confounded drum, but no one can understand what he is trying to say."

"But what's wrong with him? Don't the doctors know?" asked Johnny. Dr. Coote was not one of his closest friends, but he liked the old man, and the news of his illness upset Johnny.

"The doctors don't know, as a matter of fact," muttered the professor. "Bunch of quacks! It sounds as if my old friend is showing all the mental symptoms of a stroke, but the doctor told me there is no sign of paralysis or any of the other physical symptoms of stroke. They are calling it a 'nervous breakdown' for the time being. I don't know—poor Charley has always been high-strung, and I guess it's possible that he worried himself into a crack-up over that idiotic toy drum."

"What are you going to do, Professor?"

Professor Childermass drank the last of his coffee. "I hardly know," he admitted. "I honestly don't see anything much that I *can* do. But Charley is an old and dear friend, and I do not have many of them left. I hate to think of him all alone in that hospital. His wife has been dead for years, you know, and they had no children. His only close relative is his sister, and she lives in California or some such barbaric state. So I am the only one who can rally 'round in an emergency. I would go up tonight, but the doctor told me that although Charley is just about helpless, he is in no immediate danger. I'll drive up to see him this Friday after class and stay until Sunday. If nothing else, at least I can show Charley that I am thinking of him, and possibly he will be a bit more lucid with me around than he has been with all those strangers."

Johnny felt embarrassed. All at once his problem of what to wear to a stupid Halloween party seemed unimportant. He said, "Professor, can I—I mean, may I go with you? I like Dr. Coote too, and I'd like to keep you company, if you don't mind my tagging along."

Professor Childermass smiled. He liked very few people the way he liked Johnny Dixon. Johnny was brainy and resourceful and kindhearted—just as he himself had been at that age. And Johnny had a way of making sensible conversation and asking the right questions at the right time, which were gifts that the professor always admired. He said, "If you really want to go, John Michael, I shall be happy to have you along. Fortunately, that blasted young fool Duquesne has recovered from the vapors and brain fever, and he will be taking his worthless students off my hands tomorrow." Professor Childermass hesitated. Then he said, in a very serious voice, "It would be unfair of me to allow you to go along without saying this, John. Be prepared for the worst."

Johnny felt his heart thump. "What do you mean?"

The professor shook his head and sighed. "I mean that Charley is a tougher old bird than you would think, but he is an *old* bird. He—well, John, to be honest, he may not make it." For a second the professor just sat at the table looking bleak. Then he began to cry. Johnny swallowed hard at a lump in his throat. For the first time, he realized just how sick Dr. Coote must really be.

CHAPTER THREE

Johnny easily talked his grandparents into letting him go to New Hampshire with the professor. "My stars, Johnny, of course you can go," Gramma said, her wrinkled face showing her sympathy. "I dunno what life would be like if folks didn't stick by their friends. An' who knows, maybe a visit might do Dr. Coote a world o' good. He always seemed t' like you."

So it was all arranged. On Friday as soon as he got out of school, Johnny climbed into the professor's maroon Pontiac, and they set off for Portsmouth, New Hampshire, where Dr. Coote was hospitalized. They drove steadily north, the professor talking the whole way. He had been on the phone to Dr. Coote's doctors, and although the news was not good, at least the old man was holding his own. Even that slender ray of hope put the professor into a slightly more optimistic frame of mind as the car careened along. Johnny frequently had to fight to keep from crying out in alarm as the Pontiac wove in and out of traffic. Professor Childermass was a miserable driver, and on five or six occasions he came close to sideswiping another car or running off the road. He never seemed to notice these hairbreadth escapes himself, and he chatted away nonchalantly the whole time.

As usual, the professor refused to stop and ask for directions, insisting that he was old enough to find his way around a dinky little New Hampshire town. They came to the outskirts of Portsmouth, and the professor took a few turns that he thought were familiar. He quickly got lost. The Pontiac roamed streets of boxy white frame and gray clapboard buildings, passed the tall, narrow mansions of Strawberry Banke, and wandered near the Piscataqua River. They drove aimlessly around Portsmouth for almost an hour before Professor Childermass threw in the towel. With a furious expression he pulled into a service station and stopped the car with a screech of brakes. At once a skinny young man in a gray baseball cap and grease-stained gray coveralls trotted out and stooped by the driver's window. "Can I fill 'er up for ya?" he asked, smiling cheerfully.

"You may not," said the professor coldly. "I suspect that this particular brand of gasoline is filthy with pollutants and automotive poisons. If I allowed you to put so much as one teaspoonful in my car, the engine would no doubt scream in agony, give a feeble kick, and expire altogether. Moreover, I despise your company's inane commercial jingle and deplore the tasteless so-called comedian it sponsors on television. However, since you are so eager to help, you might as well tell me where in this dreary burg I could find a sinkhole of suffering misnamed Mercy Hospital!"

The young man's eyes grew round and his mouth hung open. He gulped a couple of times. "Sure," he said. He pointed with a shaking finger. "'S easy. Just turn right at the corner ahead, then go straight until ya come t' the first stoplight. Turn left at the light an' go about a quarter of a mile. The hospital will be the big brick building off to your right."

"Don't you *dare* tell me I can't miss it!" thundered the professor.

"Uh, s-sure, y' can m-miss it if y' want to," stammered the young man. He stood wiping his face with an oily pink rag as the professor floored the accelerator and the Pontiac roared out of the service-station lot. Despite his worries about Dr. Coote's condition, Johnny got a case of the giggles. It was always interesting to witness someone's first introduction to the professor.

Without any more trouble they found the hospital, a red-brick relic of the 1890s, three stories tall with a green tile roof. The windows all had arched tops, and round fanlights crowned all the doors. In the deepening dusk many of the windows glowed with soft yellow light. The professor parked the Pontiac, and they hurried toward the old building. By now the sun had vanished behind a bank of ragged gray clouds, and a chilly wind had sprung up, rattling the few dead leaves left on the oaks and maples that bordered the parking lot.

"Uh-oh," Johnny said as they went in. "We're about five minutes too late, Professor." He pointed to a black-bordered sign posted on the wall just inside the entrance:

MERCY HOSPITAL
Visiting Hours
10:00–12:00 AM
2:00–5:00 PM

The professor snorted. "Bureaucratic blathering. Never mind that hogwash. We shall see Charley, or my name is not Roderick Childermass. Follow me!"

Sure enough, Professor Childermass bullied his way past the nurses' station, discovered where his friend was, and led the way up to the third floor of the north wing. Although Dr. Coote was not exactly wealthy, he had a comfortable income and considerable savings, and the university provided him with an excellent medical insurance plan. They found him all alone in a private room, sleeping propped up in bed. His face had a miserable expression of suffering, even in sleep. With a worried glance at Johnny, the professor said, "I noticed the nurse is about to serve dinner to the patients. Why don't we stay in the waiting room until after Charley eats?"

Johnny realized that his friend's haggard appearance

bothered the professor. It upset him too, so he swallowed and whispered, "Fine."

They paused in the hallway while the professor spoke to a young nurse who was trundling a cart loaded with dinner trays. Then they went down the hall to the waiting room. Framed prints of trains by the New Hampshire artist Arch McDonnell hung on the walls, and two dingy windows looked out over the parking lot. A threadbare brown carpet, spotted with cigarette burns and splashed with old coffee stains, covered the floor. One drooping, dusty rubber tree, a couple of broken-down sofas, a few dilapidated armchairs, and a table holding a couple of ashtrays and several years of *National Geographic* furnished the room.

The only other person there was a quiet young man of twenty-five or so. He was slim with black, curly hair and wore a gray suit, a white button-down shirt, and a black tie. A charcoal-gray overcoat lay folded in the seat beside him. A couple of empty paper coffee cups rested on the table before him. He was reading an old magazine and hardly glanced up as Johnny and the professor entered. The professor immediately sank into one of the armchairs and took out a black-and-gold box of his Balkan Sobranie cigarettes. He lit one and smoked impatiently, drumming his fingers almost silently on the arm of his chair. He hummed a fidgety, unmelodic tune, as he often did when trying to control his temper.

Johnny settled into a chair and picked up a dog-eared issue of *National Geographic*. For a few minutes he read about turtle fishing in the Leeward Islands, but he could not keep his mind on the article, so after a little while he tossed the magazine aside. "Professor," he said, "what do you think is wrong with Dr. Coote? Except for his expression, he didn't look so bad to me."

The young man looked up in surprise. His eyes were a very dark brown. Professor Childermass ground out the stub of his cigarette. "I haven't the faintest idea, John Michael," he muttered. "But I agree with you. Though he is obviously ailing, Charley looks robust enough physically. If the fool doctors don't kill him in this so-called hospital, that is."

"Excuse me," said the young man, getting to his feet. "I didn't mean to eavesdrop, but did I hear you mention Dr. Charles Coote?"

Johnny noticed that his voice was deep and pleasant, with a slight trace of foreign accent. Professor Childermass stared at the interloper. "Dr. Charles Coote is one of my oldest friends," he said in a blunt, unfriendly voice. "And what, pray tell, is *your* interest in him?"

"I'm sorry," said the young man placatingly. "Let me introduce myself. I am Todd Lamort, a student at the University of New Hampshire. Dr. Coote is directing my thesis in folklore." Lamort gave them an anxious smile. Then he added, "Uh, I organized a blood drive, just in case he needs a transfusion. About a dozen of his students came in with me, and we each donated a pint of blood today. The nurse said I could hang around a little while, to see him if he wakes up."

Professor Childermass sniffed. "Very kind of you, I'm sure," he muttered. "I can just imagine what *my* students would do if I were in a similar fix. Donate strychnine and arsenic, probably." He introduced himself and Johnny.

"I'm pleased to meet you both," said young Lamort, his face set in that nervous smile. "I'm a very eager student, as Dr. Coote knows. I hope he recovers soon so that we can continue with my studies."

Johnny bit his lip. There was something about Lamort's smooth voice and strained expression that bothered him a little, but then he was upset about Dr. Coote's illness. "Have you been here long?" Johnny asked him. "How is Dr. Coote?"

Lamort glanced at him. "I've been at his bedside most of the day," he said, "but he is not making much sense, to tell you the truth." The young man looked at his wristwatch. "It's getting late, and I really have to go. Professor Childermass, could I give you my telephone number? You might call me if there is any way I can help."

"Certainly," said Professor Childermass, genuinely touched that a student could be so thoughtful. Lamort scribbled his name and number on the back of one of the professor's business cards and said good-bye.

After the young man had left, the professor murmured, "Well, well, I envy Charley if all his students are as considerate as— Good God!"

A terrible, bloodcurdling scream had ripped through

the air. Johnny felt cold chills. It was Dr. Coote's voice! Johnny and the professor ran to Dr. Coote's room. They rushed in to find him sitting up in bed, staring wildly. His dinner tray had fallen, spilling chicken soup and Jell-O on the floor. "Roderick!" he gasped. "Keep her away! Keep her away from me!"

"Who?" asked Professor Childermass, sounding bewildered.

"The woman in black! The bride of the devil! She flies through the midnight air like contagion! Roderick, help me! She's behind the boy! She's after my soul!"

Johnny yelled in alarm as Dr. Coote tried to leap out of bed. The effort was too much for the old man. He fell back heavily, in a dead faint. Professor Childermass tried to wrestle his falling body onto the bed, so he would not hit the floor.

Johnny could not help looking over his shoulder. For a second time he felt ice in his veins. Down at the end of the hall stood a squat, toadlike figure. It was an ancient woman, broad and heavy, wearing a black dress and a black scarf from which straggled long, tangled gray hair. Her ugly, wide-mouthed face held a leer of malevolent triumph. Before Johnny could cry out, she whirled and pushed her way through the door at the end of the hall. Then two nurses came running in, and Johnny had no chance to tell the professor what he had seen.

CHAPTER FOUR

Not long after Johnny saw the terrible woman in black, Dr. Coote revived for just a few moments. He clutched at the professor's arms and said hoarsely, "The spirit sleeps under running water. The *loas* rest at the bottoms of rivers for a whole year, and they can harm no one, and no one can harm them!" Dr. Coote gave a ghastly laugh. "I've fooled her, or else she would have killed me by now. Cut the cord, Roderick. For God's sake, find the doll. And don't let them cut your hair! It's *voudon*, I tell you! The serpent and the Baron and the walking dead!" Johnny, standing ignored at the foot of the bed, shivered to hear such babbling. A heavy, gray-haired doctor came in and gave Dr. Coote an injection. Little by little the old man calmed down and fell into a deep sleep. The doctor ordered the professor and Johnny out of the room, and for once the professor gave up without much of a protest.

After about ten or fifteen minutes, the doctor found them in the waiting room. "He will sleep all night now," he said. "So you two might as well go home. Are you family, by any chance?"

"No. Friends," said Professor Childermass, and he explained that Dr. Coote had no close family nearby. He added, "Johnny and I will be staying in Charley's house for the next two nights. I have a spare key. You can reach us there if you need to get in touch."

The doctor nodded, and the professor and Johnny left the hospital. By now night had fallen, and with it had come a distinct chill. They hurried to the Pontiac, and the professor screeched the tires as he pulled out of the hospital parking lot. "As soon as the engine warms up, I'll switch on the heater," he said. "It's about ten miles to Charley's house."

"Professor, I think I saw the woman who scared Dr. Coote," Johnny said. He described the haggy old woman he had glimpsed at the end of the hall.

Professor Childermass snorted. "Probably a cleaning lady, from your description. I have noticed that hospitals are particularly apt to hire the most insanitary-looking individuals for cleaning and food preparation. I wouldn't worry about witches if I were you. It's more likely that poor Charley has just had a nervous collapse from an unhealthy preoccupation with that dratted drum. If I can find the wretched thing, I shall take a hatchet to it."

They drove toward Durham on Route 4, past the barn-yard smell of the university dairy, through the university itself, and at last into the driveway of Dr. Coote's old Victorian house on Pierce Street. It was two stories tall, with weathered clapboard walls, a mansard roof with three dormers, and a two-car garage. Johnny opened the garage door and the professor managed to maneuver the Pontiac into the garage without knocking any major parts off the car or the house or Dr. Coote's old blue Chevrolet. A locked door led from the garage into the house, but since the professor had only a key to the front door, they closed the garage and went to the front of the house.

For a few moments the professor fumbled with the key and swore under his breath because it was too dark for him to see the keyhole. Then he turned the key in the lock and pushed the door open. He felt around on the wall for a light switch and clicked it on. Dr. Coote had lived all alone for years, but he was a fussy old man who liked everything just so, and the house normally was neat and orderly. Normally—but not now. Johnny gasped. The hall closet stood open, and coats, hats, and umbrellas lay scattered on the floor. Professor Childermass cursed and strode into the chilly house.

Someone had gone through every room, pulling things down, strewing books and photographs of Dr. Coote's field trips all over the house. "What happened?" Johnny asked.

"Obviously, vandals have broken in," growled the old man.

"Professor, do you think they might have been—well, looking for something? Like the drum?"

The professor glared at Johnny. "Nonsense! It was probably just a gang of young hooligans ransacking the place. Let me get the furnace started so we won't freeze, and then we'll see about setting this place to rights."

The furnace was in the basement. The old house had once been heated by coal, but like many other people, Dr. Coote had converted his furnace to burn oil. Professor Childermass checked to make sure it had plenty of fuel, then fired it up. As soon as the furnace was going, he prowled through the basement, which was full of deep black shadows cast by a single bare bulb. "Aha!" he said, pausing before what had once been the coal bin. "Just as I thought."

"What is it?" Johnny asked, coming up behind him.

"Here is where the pests got in. See how the door to the coal chute is ajar? Well, we'll soon put an end to that." He went upstairs and came down again in a few minutes with a hammer and a handful of long nails. He drove these into the coal-chute door, and soon he had sealed it shut. "Now let's clean up a little, and then we'll see about having some dinner. I'm famished."

They could do very little with the downstairs part of the house that evening, but the professor did tidy up Dr. Coote's bedroom, where even the sheets had been torn off the bed. He patiently picked up shirts and trousers from the floor and hung them in the closet. He matched scattered shoes into pairs and placed them on a shoe tree, and he replaced stacks of paper, pens, and books on Dr. Coote's desk. Meanwhile, Johnny cleaned up the guest bedroom across the hall. The mess there was not as bad, and he finished before the professor did. He came back in just as the professor patted the last wrinkles out of the remade bed. Johnny heard a trickle of water. "Is someone in the bathroom?" he asked nervously.

"No," said Professor Childermass. "It's just Charley's ancient plumbing. The toilet is dribbling, and I wouldn't know how to begin repairing it. I'd hate to have his water bill!" He pulled his pocketwatch out. "It's almost seven-thirty, and I'm starving. There's a small restaurant not far from here that serves a good hamburger. I suggest we go there for dinner, and then tomorrow we'll repair the rest of the damage to Charley's house."

Something had been bothering Johnny. He bit his lip, and then he said, "Professor, don't you think we should call the cops? Aren't you supposed to report burglars?"

Professor Childermass clicked his watch shut. "Knowing the quality of the police around here, I wouldn't dream of reporting this to them," he said. "Why, they have frequently given me traffic tickets that I certainly did not deserve! No, I think we've got matters under control now."

They drove to the restaurant, which was full of university students, many of them wearing goofy-looking blue-and-white freshman beanies. The crowd was noisy and cheerful, and the hamburgers were indeed very tasty. That evening the professor slept in Dr. Coote's bedroom, while Johnny stayed across the hall in the guest room. It took a long time for Johnny to fall asleep. When he did, he kept waking up after uneasy dreams of the drum and the symbols on it: The white skull and the red drop of blood were especially prominent. But most of all, he dreamed of the repulsive old woman. He would wake, fall asleep, and dream again. Sometimes he dreamed that he came home from school and went into the kitchen, and when Gramma turned around from the stove, she had the horrible old woman's leering face. Other times he dreamed that he was at the Halloween party, and the old woman was there. When the time came for everyone to unmask, she took off her face, eyes and nose and all, and revealed a living, grinning skull beneath. Johnny got very little sleep that night.

When Professor Childermass called the hospital early the next morning, he was told Dr. Coote was still sleeping, so the professor said that he and Johnny would visit that afternoon. After he hung up the phone, the professor said, "Help me set the kitchen straight, and I'll scare up breakfast. We may as well use Charley's provisions as let them spoil in the refrigerator." After considerable tidying, the two settled down to a breakfast of eggs, pancakes, and hot cocoa. That fortified them for a long morning of replacing all the items the vandals had pulled down.

Oddly, nothing was broken. Not a dish, not a picture, not a mirror. Everything merely lay in confusion on the floors, and picking it all up took hours. They left for the hospital in early afternoon, stopped for a quick lunch at a diner, and arrived just in time to see young Todd Lamort coming out of Dr. Coote's room. "How is he today?" asked Professor Childermass.

Lamort looked startled to see them, but he quickly recovered and said, "Uh—about the same, I'm afraid. I have to study for an exam, so I'm leaving now. Be sure to call if there is anything I can do."

"Wait a second," said Professor Childermass. "Now that you mention it—I suppose you are renting a place to live?"

Lamort looked puzzled. "Yes, that's right. I am renting an old farmhouse. It isn't fancy, but it is close to the campus."

"May I ask you to consider staying in Dr. Coote's house for a while? Johnny and I were there last night, and we saw some signs of interlopers. I think it would be good to keep the house occupied. You could stand guard, and in return live there rent free. I'm sure Charley wouldn't mind."

Lamort licked his lips. "Uh, thanks. That's very kind. I'll think it over. Call me before you leave town, and we'll settle the matter. I really have to go now—I've got some studying to do."

Professor Childermass watched the young man hurry away. "If only we had more like him," he said with a sigh. "Come on, John Michael. Let's see how our friend is doing today."

Dr. Coote was somewhat better, but not much. He was awake, but his conversation was disjointed and rambling, as if he could not focus his mind on any one thing. He muttered about the Priests of the Midnight Blood, about someone trying to steal his soul, about other frightening matters. To Johnny it all made very little sense. Every now and then the old man would give that terrible chuckle and rave about a running stream and about trapping a spirit. "No communication there, you know," he said with a wink at them. "Keep an Invisible in the dark long enough, and it turns on its master. The tyrant must fall. And the Baron defeats even the proudest of tyrants. The drum, the drum. He was a rebel, you know, in New Orleans. *She* did him in, the crone who flies in the night. Lost, lost!" And he would sob in a heartbroken way.

Johnny felt terrible. The same doctor they had seen the night before looked in around four thirty. Dr. Coote lay semiconscious and delirious, mumbling words too softly for anyone to make out. "No improvement since yesterday," said the doctor with a sigh. He appeared to be honestly concerned. He had a square jaw, close-cut gray hair, and a brushy gray mustache. He stroked his mustache as he nodded at Johnny and the professor. "I wish I had better news for you, but your friend Dr. Coote has been in this state since I first saw him on Monday. And we can't seem to come up with a diagnosis."

For a short time he talked with the professor and Johnny, and then he left. When visiting hours ended, the professor and Johnny drove back to Durham, where they ate at another restaurant before returning to Dr. Coote's house. Professor Childermass took the lead in going inside, as if he half expected more intruders. None materialized, and he and Johnny spent some time in the living room watching westerns on television. They decided to turn in early. Both were in bed by nine thirty.

Exhausted from the excitement of the previous night and the cleaning and picking up of the day, Johnny fell asleep almost at once. This time he did not have any terrible dreams, and he slept soundly until well past three o'clock in the morning. Suddenly, though, he woke up, sure he had heard a noise. He lay awake in bed, straining his ears. He could hear the house creaking, the way all old houses do. He could even hear the faraway tinkle of water running in the leaky toilet in the bathroom across the hall. But he could not hear anything that sounded odd or threatening. Still, he thought, he had better check it out. He got out of bed, put on his glasses and slippers, and pulled his apple-green terrycloth bathrobe around him. He crept softly downstairs, feeling nervous. Johnny was a timid and cautious boy, and normally he would never venture into danger. However, he had spent the night at Dr. Coote's house a couple of times before, and it was familiar to him. Besides, he had not heard anything that sounded dangerous.

He patrolled the washroom, kitchen, study, living room, and dining room. Nothing there. Doors all locked tight. He was about to go upstairs again when he realized he had not checked the cellar door in the kitchen. He went there and turned the knob of the cellar door. To his surprise the door swung open, though he was almost certain that the professor had locked it after lighting the furnace. Johnny hesitated to go inside the cellar because he remembered that the only light down there was a bare hanging bulb. He did not want to stumble around in the dark, trying to find it.

Just as he decided that he had better go back upstairs and wake the professor, he heard something. A creak, stealthy and quiet, coming from the darkness of the cellar stairs. Johnny backed away. A dark figure moved in the blackness inside the cellar door. Johnny opened his mouth to shout a warning.

Someone lurched into the room, and the warning froze like ice in Johnny's throat.

A man had staggered out of the cellar. His hair was black, and his face white and bloodless, as if made of marble. His cheeks were sunken, his lips purple and pulled back from yellow teeth. But his eyes . . . they were the worst of all. They were filmed and blind, the cloudy color of light-blue chalk. Rimmed with fine black dirt, the eyes stared sightlessly straight ahead. He wore a black suit, and he thrust his arms before him, like someone sleepwalking. The appearance of anyone from that dark cellar would have shocked Johnny, but this man terrified him. This man was dead.

The figure shambled forward, reaching for Johnny. Johnny finally screamed and turned to run. Too late! He felt a dead hand close on the back of his robe. The zombie held Johnny in an unearthly grip.

CHAPTER FIVE

Johnny's scream woke Professor Childermass from a sound sleep. The professor fumbled for his glasses, but he could not even find the bedside table. Then he remembered that he was not in his own home, and Dr. Coote's table was on the opposite side of the bed. The professor found the lamp, switched it on, and grabbed his glasses just as he heard Johnny scream again. "What in the name of heaven?" mumbled the old man as he tugged on his trousers and shoved his feet into his slippers. He ran downstairs.

The kitchen was empty, but the cellar door stood ajar. Just as the professor reached the door, he heard a long shuddery screech of nails. Someone was breaking in! Professor Childermass looked wildly around the kitchen for a weapon. A large cast-iron frying pan was hanging on the wall. He snatched it and hurried to the cellar door. Professor Childermass blundered down the cellar stairs, the frying pan held in his right hand, his right elbow bent and ready to strike. He flailed about with his left hand, hunting the chain hanging from the lightbulb.

A louder screech came from the coal chute. And another sound too: Johnny's muffled whimpering, as if someone had clamped a hand over the boy's mouth. Just then the professor finally found the lightbulb and jerked the chain. Yellow light flooded the cellar. Long black shadows danced crazily as the bulb swung back and forth on its wire. And in the sudden glare, Professor Childermass saw someone squirm up through the coal-chute opening. All he could see were long, thin legs clad in black trousers—and a couple of pale bare feet. "Johnny!" the professor cried. "Are you there?"

"Yes!" The answering yell was faint because it came from outside. The long legs disappeared as the intruder climbed out through the coal chute. The professor realized that he would never fit through the opening, so he turned and ran upstairs and fumbled with the kitchen-door lock. He grabbed his car keys from his pocket as he burst out into the garage. He had a powerful flashlight in the trunk of his Pontiac. He had to set the frying pan down and find the right key, and all the while he was picturing the most awful things happening to his young friend. At last the trunk swung open. The professor switched on the flashlight, and in its beam he saw a much better weapon than a frying pan. He picked up the curved L shape of his tire iron and again ran around to the back.

A light frost lay on the grass in the backyard. In the glow of his flashlight the professor saw a dark trail that led through the frosty grass back toward the spirea hedge that formed the boundary between Dr. Coote's yard and that of the house behind his. Professor Childermass, shivering from the cold, ran along the track. He squeezed through the stiff branches of the hedge and saw a dark shape ahead of him. It was a tall, thin man, walking heavily and leaning to his left. Under his right arm dangled a shape—a shape that could be Johnny.

"Stop!" Professor Childermass yelled as he ran forward. "By heaven, sir, stop, or I shall—"

The thin man turned. The first thing the professor saw gave him a jolt of relief. The intruder carried Johnny with his right arm, and he had his left hand pressed over Johnny's mouth—but Johnny was wriggling and kicking, his green bathrobe fluttering with his struggles. He was alive! Then in the next instant the professor turned the flashlight beam onto the stranger's face and felt sudden terror.

The man was clearly dead. His eyes had lost all their luster, and his skin had the pallor of death. And yet this creature moved and walked and held Johnny in a viselike grip. With a wild cry the professor leaped forward, swinging the tire iron.

The intruder moved faster than the professor would have thought possible. The left hand let go of Johnny—

who released a long shuddering wail—and intercepted the tire iron. The weapon fell with a heavy *smack!* Yet the eerie stranger gave no indication of having felt the slightest pain. The fingers closed on the tire iron, the man gave a twisting wrench, and the professor felt the tire iron fly from his hand. The creature swung his arm in a vicious backhand swipe that surely would have knocked the professor unconscious—except that he slipped in the icy grass and fell under the blow.

The momentum of the swing moved the intruder halfway around. The professor had an inspiration. He barrel-rolled forward, coming up beside the creature, and he used the flashlight as a club. He struck as hard as he could at the back of the zombie's right knee—knowing that even the strongest person can be toppled if the knee is forced forward.

The man tumbled, thrusting his hands out. They slid across the frosty grass, and the dead man went sprawling. Johnny sprang up and tugged at the professor's arm. "Let's get outa here!" he bawled.

Professor Childermass needed no urging. He scrambled up, and together he and Johnny ran back toward Dr. Coote's house. "Go!" ordered Professor Childermass when they reached the hedge. He shoved Johnny roughly through the gap he had forced earlier. A noise came from behind him, and the professor fearfully turned the flashlight back that way. Amazingly, the flashlight bulb was still burning, and he saw the creature lurching toward him. The professor scraped through the hedges. "Get to the garage!" he yelled at Johnny. "We'll take my car!" Lights began to come on in the houses behind Dr. Coote's place as all the commotion woke people up.

Before they were halfway across the backyard, the professor heard the thrashing of the zombie coming through the hedge. He ran with all his strength, easily catching up to Johnny. They piled into the Pontiac, and the professor pulled the keys from his trouser pocket. He started the car, and the tires screamed as the car leaped back.

"Look out, Professor!" screamed Johnny. The car hit something with a sickening *thump*, and then the tires bounced over something—*thud! thud!* The professor turned on the headlights and could hardly believe what he saw. The car had knocked down the zombie, and both the rear and the front wheels had rolled over the body. But the creature rose and turned, his horrible dead face staring bleakly at them in the headlight glow. He lurched toward them.

Johnny screamed. The professor heard distant yells: "What's goin' on?" "For cryin' out loud, we're tryin' ta sleep here!" And then another sound, high and musical and sinister: the sound of a flute or pipe. And a deep regular pounding, like bare hands beating a drum in a wild rhythm. The zombie's head turned. He staggered away and disappeared into the night.

For a few moments the professor sat behind the wheel,

the Pontiac's engine humming. He took long, shuddering breaths. Then he turned to Johnny. "I believe someone called the—the *thing* off," he panted.

Johnny's teeth were chattering. He stammered, "Th-that *thing* w-was a zombie, Professor!"

"Calm down," said the professor. "Whatever it was, it's gone now. Well, shall we return to Duston Heights right now, John Michael? Or shall we go back inside and see how that ghastly creature got in?"

Johnny was trembling. "He was there the whole time, Professor," he gasped. "He must have been hidin' in the cellar all along. Maybe behind the furnace, or under the stacks of old newspapers an' junk. It didn't break *in*—it was breakin' *out* when you came."

"Was it?" said the professor. "Well, that settles it." He put the Pontiac in gear and rolled it into the garage. "I'll be dipped in bread crumbs and French fried if I'll let anyone, living or dead, make a fool of me. And somebody owes me a tire iron too!"

The two of them got out and carefully locked the garage door, and together they went down into the cellar. Sure enough, the professor could clearly see that the zombie had yanked the cover off the coal-chute opening from inside. A couple of the nails had been left in the frame, and in climbing out the creature had bent them. Grumbling under his breath, the professor fetched a hammer and long nails and fastened the coal-chute door back into place. Then he hunted around until he found an old broom. He sawed the broom head off, and with a couple of pieces of board he nailed the handle into place as a brace against the cover.

They looked behind the furnace and found a faint impression in the dust where the zombie must have waited. "Somebody sent our friend in," muttered the professor, "and then left him here like a time bomb. I'll bet you my Pontiac to a dried-up jelly doughnut that I know what he was after too. It was that cursed drum!"

"Wh-what do we do now, Professor?" stammered Johnny. He was terrified. He remembered all too well the zombie's clammy grip and empty gaze. He knew he would see them again in his nightmares.

The professor took a deep breath. "Well," he said, "it's only three or four hours before dawn. Let's make a tour of the house and make sure we don't find any other nasty little surprises."

They found nothing else out of the ordinary, and they looked everywhere that a person—or a zombie—could possibly lurk. They had breakfast at sunup, packed their bags, and loaded the Pontiac. At eight o'clock Professor Childermass made a telephone call, talked for a few minutes, then came back to the kitchen table looking smug. "I believe I have taken care of a rather bad problem," he said. "I telephoned young Todd Lamort and got him to agree to the offer I made. He says he will stay here in Charley's house for the time being. He will keep an eye on things, and whoever broke in will think twice with a young, strong man in residence."

"Did—did you tell him about—" Johnny could not finish.

"Certainly not," said the professor. "However, I did warn him that burglars have been a problem. He says he will be on his toes, and I believe we can trust him. I certainly wish we had more young men like him."

An hour or so later Todd Lamort showed up. The professor took him on a tour of the house and turned his key over to the young man. After giving Lamort his address and phone number, the professor said, "I shall telephone every other day or so to check on things. But as long as you stay alert, there shouldn't be any problems."

Then Johnny and the professor drove back to Duston Heights. Gramma and Grampa Dixon noticed how subdued Johnny was, but he explained that Dr. Coote's illness had upset him.

Days passed, and the professor kept pretty much to himself. Johnny told Fergie that he definitely would *not* dress up as a zombie. In the end he went to the Halloween party as a tramp, just as Grampa had suggested. Fergie showed up as a zombie, but in his green greasepaint and torn old clothes, he was certainly not as scary as the real thing had been. And at least his father had refused to lend him any rubber fishing worms.

Johnny told Fergie about his adventure, because Fergie was the only person he could talk to about such things. Fergie listened as the two of them sat at a table in Peter's

Sweet Shop, sipping chocolate malteds. Fergie whistled in an impressed way at Johnny's description. "Wowee, Dixon," he said. "I dunno why you didn't go outa your ever-lovin' mind! Course, it was probably just some guy tryin' ta scare ya—"

"It was not!" whispered Johnny fiercely. "Fergie, I saw his horrible gray face and felt his cold, clammy hands. This guy was *dead*!"

"Okay, okay," replied Fergie with an irritating smirk. "Keep your hair on, big John. Just for the sake of argument, let's say it really was a zombie. So what's the professor gonna do about this, huh?"

Johnny shook his head. "He hasn't told me. And when I ask him, he just tells me to mind my own beeswax. But I know he's been up to Portsmouth again, an' he's been talkin' to some other college professor on the phone a lot."

"I betcha he's learnin' how to handle zombies," mused Fergie. "I wonder how ya kill them. A stake through the heart? Nah, that's vampires—John baby, ya listenin'?"

Johnny's jaw had dropped open, and he stared through the window in frozen terror. At last he croaked, "It's her! See? There she is—it's *her*. She's here in Duston Heights!"

Fergie craned his neck around and stared out through the front window of the Sweet Shop. He saw a shapeless, dumpy old woman standing at the curb, carrying a shopping bag. She wore a black coat and a black scarf, and long, gray hair straggled down across her shoulders.

Then she crossed the street and turned a corner. "So who is it, Dixon?" asked Fergie. "Looked like th' devil's granma to me—"

Johnny jumped up out of his seat. "We gotta tell the professor," he said. "C'mon!"

The two ran all the way to Fillmore Street, but they found the professor's house empty, and his car was nowhere in sight. "Oh, no," Johnny said. "Well, as soon as he comes back, we have to tell him. Want to come in for a while?"

"Sure," said Fergie. "How 'bout some poker, John baby? Last time I looked, ya owed me two an' a half million bucks."

"Okay," said Johnny, but without much enthusiasm.

"Hiya, Fergie," said Gramma as they walked in. "Say, Johnny, look what I got." She held up a white cardboard box with a clear cellophane top. The box held a hairbrush and a hand mirror, both of them in silver-colored frames with white porcelain ovals on the backs. A red-and-green pattern of vines and roses decorated the ovals.

"It's great," Johnny said.

"An' best of all, it's free," replied Gramma, smiling broadly. "Darndest thing y' ever heard of. This ol' lady comes t' th' door sellin' brushes and such, an' she says she'll trade this for my old hairbrush. Beats me how anybody expects t' make a livin' if she does everybody that way!"

Johnny felt cold. "Gramma, what did this old lady look like?" he asked.

His grandmother laughed. "Well, she was sure no bathin' beauty! She looked kinda like a big toad, t' tell ya the truth. She had long stringy gray hair an' she wore this awful ol' black scarf, an' she talked funny. I could hardly unnerstan' her—say, Johnny, you all right?"

Johnny had almost fainted. The terrible old woman knew where he lived. Would the zombie turn up next? Or did she have something much worse in store for the Dixon family?

CHAPTER SIX

As the first week of November passed, nothing much changed. Professor Childermass took the news about the weird woman with some impatience. He had not seen the toadlike figure in the hospital, and he grumbled that Johnny was making a mountain out of a molehill. "Probably she's just what she says," he muttered. "A deranged Fuller Brush lady or something. But I'll be on the lookout for her, if it will make you feel any better." In the following days neither the professor nor Johnny saw anything more of the mysterious woman. Worse, the professor became even more secretive than he had been, and with one exception he told Johnny almost nothing.

The one thing that he did talk about was the zombie. On a chilly Saturday morning the professor invited

Johnny over for a game of chess. As usual, they played in the professor's cluttered second-floor study, but the old man's mind was not really on the game, and he lost his queen after only about half an hour of play. Then he pushed back from his desk, cleared his throat, and said, "I've been debating whether or not to show you something, John. I have decided that not only can you take it, but you will have to see it. I did not get as close a look at—ahem!—our midnight visitor as you did."

He opened a desk drawer and took out a folded newspaper. He pointed to a small, grainy photograph. "Recognize this fellow?"

Johnny shivered. The face in the photograph was lean and long, with gaunt cheeks, a high forehead, and deepset eyes. "Yeah, I recognize him," said Johnny. "He's the zombie."

"I thought so." With a grim smile, the professor tossed the paper over to Johnny.

Johnny read the story. It was an obituary for a Mr. Jacques Dupont. He had been a retired merchant living in Portsmouth, and he had died—Johnny blinked—a week before the chilling encounter in Dr. Coote's house. "What does it mean, Professor?" asked Johnny.

"It means the worst kind of voodoo," growled Professor Childermass. "Sinful sorcery, nefarious necromancy, and malevolent magic!" But that was all he would say. When Johnny asked if he had heard any news about Dr. Coote, the professor sighed. "Yes, and it is all bad," he said. "Charley was jabbering nonsense, but at least he was awake. Yesterday he fell unconscious and lapsed into a coma. The doctors are feeding him through a tube."

Johnny's heart sank. He began to fear that the old man did not have a fighting chance. The rest of his visit with the professor was quiet and bleak.

Fergie was no help at all when Johnny talked to him about the dead Mr. Dupont. He refused to believe that the dead could really and truly walk, and even when Johnny insisted that the professor had seen the zombie too, Fergie just smirked. The two of them did go to the public library to see if they could learn anything about the dark secrets of voodoo, but they found only a couple of books on the subject. One of them, *Tell My Horse*, was by a woman named Zora Neale Hurston, who had spent time in Jamaica, Haiti, New Orleans, and other places where sorcerers did voodoo magic. The only other book the boys could find was *Hayti, or the Black Republic*, by Sir Spenser St. John. Both volumes discussed zombies, but they were not really much help. Fergie read in one of them that salty food would break the spell that animated the dead bodies. A zombie that tasted salt would remember that it was dead and would burrow down into the ground until it came to rest in its own tomb. Fergie thought that was a hilarious notion, and he whispered to Johnny that he should have offered old Mr. Dupont a bag of Lay's potato chips. Just saying that gave Fergie such a bad case of snickering that the librarian came by, frowning, and asked the boys to leave. Johnny checked out both books, but they added very little to his under-standing of exactly what he and the professor had encountered.

Days passed, and then the fourth week in November arrived. Both Fergie and Johnny would get a Thanks-giving holiday from Wednesday until the following Mon-day. On Tuesday morning Johnny came downstairs for breakfast to find Gramma sitting in a kitchen chair, pant-ing. "What's wrong, Gramma?" asked Johnny, anxiously. He thought of the terrible time when Gramma had had a brain tumor, and he worried that maybe she had an-other one.

She gave him a tight, pained smile. "Dunno. Just got kinda short o' breath. I'll be all right in a minute, but do you suppose you could make your own breakfast?"

"Do you want me to get Grampa?" Johnny asked.

Gramma made a face. "I guess so," she muttered. "Course, he'll haul me off to the doctor right away. Not a thing in the world wrong with me—just gettin' old, I expect."

By the time Johnny got Grampa into the kitchen, Gramma was better. She was right about the doctor's visit, though. Grampa phoned Doc Schermerhorn and told him he would drive Gramma over that morning for a checkup. Meanwhile, Johnny got out a box of cornflakes and made himself two pieces of toast.

He worried about his grandmother all during school, but when he got home, she seemed more or less her old self. "Slept kinda bad last night," she said. "Anyway, the doc couldn't find anything wrong with me that he didn't already know about."

That night Duston Heights got a little powdering of snow, and the next day Fergie came over early. The snow was too thin for sledding and too dry for snowballs, but the two friends enjoyed walking around town and seeing how the white layer had changed everything from drab gray to sparkling white. Johnny and Fergie stopped at Peter's Sweet Shop for a quick lunch of egg-salad sand-wiches, hot cocoa, and fudge brownies with hot chocolate sauce. Then they decided to go see if Round Pond was frozen. They knew any ice would not yet be thick enough for skating, but even a skim of ice would promise winter fun to come. Fergie was a natural athlete who skated as expertly as he did any sport, and he had taught Johnny to skate well enough to enjoy himself. Even Professor Childermass liked to get out on the ice on cold winter afternoons, and for an old man he could really whiz along.

Johnny and Fergie reached the pond to find it lightly iced. They stood on the bank and tossed stones for a while. Any heavy rock crashed right through the thin layer of ice, sending waves of gray water spouting out of the hole it made, but some of the smaller pebbles went skidding across the frozen surface. The day was warming up, and already the thin dusting of snow had melted everywhere except in the shady spots. "Is there any news about Dr. Coote?" asked Fergie as he tired of tossing the rocks. He was not wearing gloves, and he stuck his red hands deep into his coat pockets.

With a sigh Johnny said, "I don't know. Professor Childermass says he's holdin' his own, but he's in a coma. That's always bad."

"Yeah," agreed Fergie. He sighed. "Well, I hate to think of old Doc Coote croakin', but if he's gonna go, I wish it would be quick."

"Fergie!" said Johnny, scandalized.

Fergie shrugged. "I just mean I don't want to think of him sufferin'. Say, what's the matter between you an' the prof, anyhow? You've said almost nothin' about him lately."

Johnny shook his head. "He's playin' everything close to his vest," he said. He explained how Professor Childermass had been making himself scarce.

Fergie turned to him with a big grin on his face. "Dixon, don'tcha see what that means?"

"It means that the professor thinks there's something dangerous goin' on," replied Johnny promptly.

"Yeah!" said Fergie. "An' that means somethin' exciting. Now, how can we cut ourselves a slice of this pie?"

Johnny just stared at his friend. "Are you *crazy?*" he demanded. "Fergie, didn't you listen to me when I told you about that dead guy? Somethin' *bad* is goin' on, an' the professor is trying to protect us!"

"Who wants to be protected, John baby?" asked Fergie teasingly. That was just like him. Johnny had to get his nerve up before he did anything risky, but Fergie always plowed straight ahead. One day, Johnny thought sourly, Fergie's enthusiasm was going to land him in trouble so deep that he would not be able to climb back out again.

They turned to go, and Johnny felt his breath catch. Standing not ten feet away from them was the old woman he had seen twice before. She wore the same clothes— a long black coat and a tattered black scarf. Her ugly, wide face was dark and weathered. Her eyes were black slits, staring out from beneath shaggy gray eyebrows. Her wrinkled mouth grinned at him, the wide lips pulled tight against her yellow teeth. "Hello, boys," she said in a nasty, low voice. Her accent made her sound like Mr. Plessy, the French-Canadian owner of Plessy's Plumbing and Hardware in Duston Heights. She took a step toward them and purred, "The old fox is cunning, no? But maybe these two fine little pups will be able to persuade him. You, the blond one! I have something special to show you."

Johnny looked wildly around. He and Fergie were all alone on the rim of the lightly frozen pond, and the awful old woman stood between them and the only avenue of escape. "Wh-what do you want?" he stammered.

"Just to show you my handiwork—look at this!" She took something out of her coat pocket. It was a flattish cloth doll, about six inches tall. It wore a blue gingham dress and a white apron, and it had gray yarn hair done up in a bun. The face was just a pink blank, but the figure was somehow very familiar to Johnny.

To his surprise and horror, Fergie laughed—a long, raucous, mocking laugh. "Lady, that's th' worst-lookin' baby doll I've ever seen! If you're sellin' it, ya better find a couple of other customers—we don't have any little sisters, an' my buddy John and me are too old t' play with dollies!"

The awful old woman did not even look at Fergie as her slitted black eyes bored straight into Johnny's. "You recognize her, no? Your *grand-mère?* Perhaps she felt a little something wrong with her health yesterday, no? And perhaps if I stick a long pin in the dolly when the sickle moon is shining, something *very* bad happens to your *grand-mère*, no?" She stalked closer and Johnny flinched, but he had nowhere to run.

She came so close that he could smell her, a dusty, dry smell, like old leaves and crisp corn husks, and all the time she purred in her menacing voice. "You tell the old man, the old fox, that Mama Sinestra wants something, the thing that his miserable friend stole from her family. If she gets it, then *poof!* your *grand-mère* and the old fox's friend, they get better. If she does not get it—then you have been warned, no?" The evil smile left her face, and she snarled, "You have one week!"

Abruptly, the woman turned and waddled away. "Hey!" Fergie shouted after her, but she did not turn her head. "C'mon!" Fergie said to Johnny. "Let's follow her!"

Johnny grabbed his friend's arm. "No, Fergie, we can't! That's a voodoo doll of Gramma! We gotta tell th' professor about this right away!"

The woman vanished into a grove of birches as Johnny and Fergie ran in another direction. The cold air burned their lungs, and both were exhausted before they reached Fillmore Street, but neither slowed. They found the professor at home, and together they panted out their weird story to him in his cluttered study. The professor got up and paced for a few minutes, finally stopping beside the stuffed owl on its round stand. He absently reached out and straightened the owl's miniature Red Sox baseball cap, which had slipped to a rakish tilt. At last the old man shook his head and muttered, "Gentlemen, this is very, very bad news. John, I suspected that the old woman might somehow be involved in all this. Now it looks as if she is forcing my hand. Well, I have learned something about the St. Ives brand of evil witchcraft, so she may have a surprise or two coming. And she has very unwisely told us who she is."

"Huh?" said Fergie, scratching his head. "She called herself Mama Sinister or somethin' crazy like that. That doesn't sound like a real name to me, Prof!"

"It isn't a real name, Byron," returned Professor Childermass. "It is a nickname. You see, the current ruler of the Caribbean island of St. Ives is a dictator named General Hippolyte LeGrande. He maintains his rule through a combination of naked military force, intimidation, and witchcraft. And guess who the head witch is?"

"Ya mean this General Whosis isn't a witch himself?" asked Fergie.

The professor scuffed through the drift of graded papers that had built up into a dune at the foot of his desk. As he sank into his chair, he said, "I don't know if he is a witch or not, but he is not the witch that the people fear."

"So who is that?" asked Johnny.

"Her name is Madame Corinne LeGrande, and she is the general's mother," said Professor Childermass, leaning back in his chair. "Now here is the sixty-four-dollar question: What nickname do you think the people of St. Ives have given her?"

"Mama Sinestra," whispered Johnny.

"Precisely," said Professor Childermass, wrinkling his face into a disapproving frown. "And she seems to be quite a piece of work. Ruthless and intelligent and as wicked as they come." He swiveled his chair so that he could look out the window, toward the Dixon house across the street. Staring out, he gave a little start, and then, with a peculiar expression, he turned back to the boys. "Gentlemen, this is gravely important. Will you give me your absolute, ironbound promise that you will not speak of this Mama Sinestra person to anyone? I mean anyone at all, mind!"

"Sure," Fergie said at once. "Everybody'd think I was hallucinatin' if I tried to describe her anyway!"

Professor Childermass nodded. "And you, John? Will you give me your promise?"

Johnny blinked. "Well—sure, Professor, if you think it's—"

"Good," said the professor briskly. He pushed himself out of his chair, which squeaked loudly. "Now, Byron, you may stay and sample a batch of my special fudge that I made this morning. John, you had better go home right now."

Johnny could hardly believe his ears. "Go *home?* B-but—"

The professor held up a warning finger. "Home. Now. This very instant." His tone allowed no argument.

Johnny went downstairs feeling hurt. Hurt and puzzled. What was the professor hiding? He certainly had not sounded very friendly. Johnny opened the front door and froze in his tracks, staring across the street at what the professor must have seen from his study window. A yellow Chevrolet, one of Duston Heights' few taxis, was just pulling away from the curb in front of the Dixon house. Standing on the sidewalk was a tall, athletic man with a weathered, craggy face. He was wearing the blue uniform of an Air Force major.

Johnny's first, happy thought was, *Dad's home!*

And his second, despairing one was, *Is Gramma dead?*

CHAPTER SEVEN

But Gramma was fine, and she fussed over Major Harrison Dixon as if he were still her little boy. For a few hours that evening Johnny forgot all about being unhappy, and even his father's frequent worried looks at Gramma did little to bring his high spirits down. "Did you tell Mom about Thanksgiving dinner tomorrow, Pop?" asked Johnny's dad that evening.

"Yep, an' she can be mad at *you* for a change," said Grampa, grinning.

"Land sakes," said Gramma in a fussy voice. "I still can't see any sense in your orderin' a turkey an' trimmin's from the *store*. Don't you want some home cookin' for a change, Harry?"

Johnny's dad laughed. "Sure," he said. "But I want

you to rest tomorrow too. So Pop and I will drive into town early and bring everything back, and the most you can do is to bake us a couple of cherry pies." He winked at Johnny. "Say, Old Scout, are those pies as good as I remember?"

Johnny blushed. "Old Scout" was a name his dad had always used for him. "They sure are," he said, and everyone laughed. It was a sound that he liked to hear.

The Dixons always had an early Thanksgiving dinner. The next day they all settled in around the table at two o'clock. Grampa gave thanks, and they dug in. Even though it had all come from a restaurant and not from Gramma's kitchen, the turkey, dressing, and trimmings tasted delicious. After dinner Johnny's dad insisted that he and Johnny would clear the table and wash the dishes, and they did. Then Gramma, who had been supervising, went upstairs for a nap, and Grampa turned on the radio to hear a football game. "Feel like taking a walk, Old Scout?" asked Major Dixon.

"Uh—sure," said Johnny. "Let me get my jacket." He ran upstairs, wondering what was up. Johnny suspected that his dad was worried about Gramma, because he had noticed how concerned the major seemed every time he glanced at the old woman. Johnny wished that he could tell his father the truth about Gramma's illness—but that would mean breaking his word to the professor. He hurried downstairs and found his dad waiting beside the front door.

Major Dixon was wearing civilian clothes, a red-plaid

flannel shirt and Levi's, and he had pulled on one of Grampa's old jackets. Johnny thought he looked older and thinner than he remembered, but he still had the same short, light-brown hair, the same ironic gray eyes, and the same lopsided grin. "Ready to go?" he asked.

The weather had changed completely. They walked down Fillmore Street toward town under a bright-blue sky and warm sunshine. All the shops were closed for the holiday, and Duston Heights looked like a ghost town. Johnny and his father walked to Johnny's school and went into the schoolyard, where they settled into the swings. Johnny began to swing, but his father just sat there. Johnny pumped a few times and felt the stomach-dropping thrill of a big swoop. For a moment he forgot all about Dr. Coote and the frightening Mama Sinestra. His father chuckled. "Swinging's like flying, you know," he said. "When I was even younger than you are now, I used to swing in the schoolyard. My toes would point up above the treetops, and I knew I wanted to be a pilot."

Johnny let the swing settle down. The chains creaked less loudly, the swing moved slower, until finally he was just sitting there beside his dad. "I'm glad you can be here through Christmas," he said. His father had told him that he would have to leave Duston Heights on December 26 to report back to his base on time.

For a few minutes Major Dixon did not respond. At last, in a serious voice, he said, "John, I want to talk to you."

Johnny swallowed. His dad had never used that man-to-man tone with him before, and Johnny sensed that something important was on his father's mind. "All right," he said.

Major Dixon smiled at him, and then he looked away. "Well, it's hard for me to put into words. It all started when your mother died. She was so young, and her death seemed so senseless that it made me angry. More angry than I had ever been. I wanted to hit back. Do you understand?"

Johnny's stomach felt fluttery, the way it had when he was swinging. "Yeah," he muttered. "I guess I sort of felt mad too."

His father nodded and sighed. "Well, unfortunately, you can't hit back at cancer. I had no way to let my anger out. Then the Korean War began, and the Air Force called me back. In an odd way that helped. I love flying, as you know. But there was something else, Johnny." Major Dixon bit his lip and then turned to his son. "You see, every time I fired at an enemy plane, or dropped a bomb, I felt that I was finally hitting back. It was crazy, but that was the way it seemed."

Johnny felt miserable. The warm, sunny day suddenly seemed cold and empty. He missed his mother terribly, and he always tried not to think too much about her, because remembering brought back the pain. But now he had to remember her. "I can understand," he said, feeling as if he were about to cry.

His dad reached out and put his hand on Johnny's shoulder, and that helped. In a soft voice Major Dixon said, "Well, that all changed after I got shot down. I was wounded, as you remember. It wasn't much, but it kept me from flying for a few months. When I got well, the Air Force needed me for transport service. I flew rations and equipment and supplies for a while—and I flew bodies."

"Bodies?" asked Johnny.

His dad took his hand off Johnny's shoulder. His craggy face had a look of deep sadness. "Yes. Bodies of the dead and bodies of the wounded. I evacuated our boys to Japan. It was—well, it was very rough, Johnny. I saw for the first time how the war was hurting so many young men. And that was when all my anger finally left me. When I saw all those boys, eighteen and nineteen years old, it suddenly hit me that I hadn't really been shooting at your mother's sickness. I had been shooting at kids. Sure, they were Korean kids, but they were no different from American kids. Once I understood that, all my hatred just dropped away."

Johnny could not think of anything to say. He stared down at the dirt beneath the swing, scuffing his toes back and forth, making little half-moon ruts in the damp, sandy soil.

"Now, John," his father said, "I want you to understand why I am still in the Air Force and not home with you. I have two reasons. First is money. I have established a special trust account for you, and I have been putting a lot of money into it. You have enough to go to any college you want. I've been sending Gramma and

Grampa money to help them out but now I can send them more. If I stay in the Air Force for just a few more years, I can retire with a nice pension and never have to worry about working again."

"And you still get to fly," said Johnny.

Major Dixon nodded. "Yes, in the meantime I get to fly. Now, the second reason is much harder for me to put into words. When I saw those dead and wounded boys, I worried about you. Five or six years from now I don't want you flown back from some senseless war, all shot up. I'm not a very great thinker, Johnny, but it seems to me that our best hope of avoiding war is to keep our country so strong that no enemy will attack us. That is why I am training pilots for the Strategic Air Command. Can you understand that?"

"I think so," Johnny said.

His dad grinned and suddenly looked years younger, just the way Johnny remembered before he had gone to war. "You're smarter than I was at your age, Son. Well, that's what I had to tell you, and now I want to ask you something. You don't have to answer right away, but think about it. You see, I'll be eligible for early retirement in about eight months. I wouldn't get my full pension, just a small one, so I would have to keep working. However, Delta Air Lines has offered me a job. It's an up-and-coming company, and it needs good pilots. If you want, I can quit the Air Force then, and you can come and live with me again."

Johnny's heart thumped. He had not expected this.

He started to say, "Yes, Dad!" Then he had second thoughts. What would saying "yes" mean? Johnny tried to control his voice. "Would we still live here, with Gramma and Grampa?" he asked.

"Well, no. You and I would have to move to Atlanta. And because I would still be away from home a lot, we would have to hire a housekeeper to stay with you."

Johnny looked away, past the school and toward St. Michael's Church. He thought of Father Higgins and Professor Childermass and Fergie and everyone else he knew in Duston Heights. He would have to leave them all behind. And what about Gramma and Grampa? It was a very difficult decision to make.

"Think it over, Old Scout," said his father. "I want to do what is best for you."

Johnny nodded, but he felt terrible. He did not want such a big responsibility, and he was confused. Confused and torn. On the one hand he had often dreamed of living with his father again, but on the other he was deeply attached to all his friends in Duston Heights and was a little afraid of moving to a strange place like Atlanta. He tried to imagine what it would be like there: hot and humid and very different, probably. The food would be unusual, and the people would talk with a strange accent. Worse, maybe they would not even like him. He had heard that Southerners often thought they were still fighting the Civil War and that they all hated "Yankees." Still, he would have a home with his father—it was all very bewildering.

"Ready to head back?" asked Major Dixon.

"Yeah," said Johnny. He slipped off the swing, and they walked up the long hill and turned onto Fillmore Street. "Dad," asked Johnny when they were still a few blocks from home, "what do *you* want to do?"

Major Dixon sighed. "Part of me wants you to stay here with Gramma and Grampa, because I worry and I know you will look after them for me. They are getting older, and Gramma's health is not very good. She looks so thin and pale. But another part of me wants you to live with me, so we can be together like a father and son should. It's all mixed up. I'll bet you figured that when you grow up, things are clear and you always know what to do."

"Yeah," admitted Johnny.

"Sorry, Old Scout. Sometimes it doesn't happen that way. Well, at least you'll have a month to think about what you would like."

As they approached his grandparents' house, Johnny saw Professor Childermass standing on the porch. The old man wore his disreputable topcoat and had his smashed-up fedora crushed onto his head, as if he had just returned from somewhere. His eyes lit up when he saw Johnny. "Ah, here you are!" he said. "Out for a constitutional?"

Major Dixon grinned. "Right, Professor. Say, why weren't you ever as friendly to me as you are to Johnny? You had me scared to death when I was in your history class."

"As well you deserved to be," growled the professor. "As I recall, Harry Dixon, you flunked the first examination in Western Civilization rather spectacularly. And don't expect me to forgive you just because you wear that ridiculous military hardware on your shoulders now! As for Johnny, he is candid when he lacks information, and always asks for assistance instead of pretending to have knowledge he does not possess. Let me quote from your examination paper—ahem!—'The Peloponnesian Wars were fought between Athens and a great general named Peloponnesium.' Disgraceful!"

Major Dixon threw his hands up and laughed. "I surrender, Professor! My gosh, it's been almost twenty years since I wrote that exam—I've never seen anybody with a memory for other people's mistakes like yours."

"The price of wisdom is eternal vigilance against ignorance," paraphrased the professor pompously. "Now, if you will allow him, Johnny is invited over to my house to sample a special Thanksgiving cake I baked just for the occasion. If you are very lucky, I may even send a slice over for you."

"It's a deal," agreed Major Dixon as he went inside.

Johnny and the professor crossed Fillmore Street. The professor acted very mysterious until they were inside his house and he had shut the door.

Then he turned and said, "Johnny, I have been consulting a friend over at Miskatonic University. Dr. Andrew Armitage is a professor who has spent many years studying sympathetic magic, the kind of enchantments that use dolls and images. He has suggested a course of action that may remove the curse that the old woman placed on your grandmother. Now, I am going to ask you to do something that may sound just a little odd. Will you trust me?"

"Sure," said Johnny. What a day this was turning out to be! Suddenly every grown-up Johnny knew seemed to be asking for his advice and help. "What do you want me to do?"

The professor's voice took on a forced lightness: "Oh, not a very great task, Johnny. It should be simple for you. In fact, I believe you are the only person who could do it."

"Do what?" asked Johnny again, bewildered.

With an uncomfortable grin, the professor said, "Nothing much. Just steal something from your grandmother for me. Now, would you like a nice cool glass of milk with your coconut-fudge cake?"

CHAPTER EIGHT

Professor Childermass sighed. "Is everyone here at last?" he asked in an exasperated tone. "I didn't want to make such a big production of this. Now pay attention, because I want to go through it only once."

It was Thanksgiving night. Father Thomas Higgins, the pastor of Johnny's church, had joined the professor, Johnny, and Fergie in the professor's living room. A friendly fire crackled in the fireplace, and everyone sat in a semicircle close by. Father Higgins, who had iron-gray hair and a permanent threatening scowl, sniffed. "Come on, Rod. You've kept us in the dark long enough. Tell us what's up."

"All in due time, Higgy," said the professor, looking mildly nettled. Except when friends his own age called him "Rod," he disliked the nickname. When Father Higgins called him that, usually it was to needle him. "Very well. At first I thought we would keep this matter only between Higgy and me, but then I realized that Johnny will be playing a part in this and Byron is also involved, so both of you deserve to know everything too. It seems to have been Byron's—ahem!—unusual drum solo that began this whole business in the first place."

"Hey," cried Fergie, sounding insulted, "don't blame *me*! I didn't know that stupid ol' bongo had a curse on it."

"Not a curse exactly," said the professor. "Something just as sinister, perhaps. Now, Higgy, you need to be brought up to date." The professor spent some time telling Father Higgins all about Dr. Coote, the drum, and the malevolent Mama Sinestra. The priest nodded with grim concentration. He had had some experience with evil spirits, so he took everything seriously. Not very long before, he himself had almost become the victim of a vengeful ghost, and only bold action on the part of the professor, Fergie, and Johnny had saved him. So he listened as the professor finished his unlikely tale: "And now this Mama Sinestra person has threatened Kate Dixon. She obviously thinks that I know where the drum is."

"I take it that Dr. Coote didn't give it to you," said Father Higgins.

"He did not," agreed the professor. "Although I'd stake my life that Charley knows more about this dark matter than anyone alive. Or *knew*, before Mama Sinestra's evil spell knocked him unconscious. However, what one person has discovered, another may learn. I have spent some weeks in research, and I honestly think I know as much regarding *voudon* as anyone else."

"Hey," said Fergie suddenly, "is that what the whatzis the old dame showed us was? A voodoo doll, the kind witch doctors stick pins in t' kill their victims?"

"It was indeed," replied Professor Childermass. "However, surprising though it may seem, I have learned that the use of such dolls is unknown in the proper Haitian practice of voodoo. But the natives of St. Ives have combined ancient European witchcraft practices—which *did* involve hex dolls—with the invocation of terrible voodoo spirits. I also found out about the drum, Byron, but I will get to that in a moment."

Johnny was worried. "Professor, can she really use that doll to kill Gramma? Isn't there anything we can do?"

The professor's expression became solemn. "The answers, John, are yes and yes. I am afraid that, under the right circumstances, the doll could indeed do your grandmother great harm, perhaps even be fatal. However, we do have some remedies. First, let me explain that the old hag who calls herself Mama Sinestra made that suspicious swap of a new hairbrush and mirror set for a reason: She needed some of Kate Dixon's hair for her cursed image. She has stuffed the doll with something—sawdust, perhaps, or cotton batting—but she has added a few strands of Kate's hair, and they give the doll its power over

John's grandmother. But there is something else at work as well. Several weeks have passed since Mama Sinestra's visit. That is because the charm takes time to prepare, and that is why she has given Kate a week before she uses the doll. It will not gain its full wicked power until the night of the new moon, next Wednesday—exactly one week from yesterday. That means that the doll cannot hurt your grandmother, John, until then."

Johnny felt confused and troubled. "But somethin' is making her feel bad right now," he said. "Somethin' that the doctor can't find!"

The professor nodded wearily. "I know the doctor has failed, but *I* can find it. The source of her trouble is hidden inside her pillow. That is why I've asked you to steal something. What I want is your grandmother's pillow, John. I found out by talking casually to your grandmother that Mama Sinestra actually accompanied her upstairs when she went to get her old hairbrush. For just a moment while your grandmother was in the bathroom, Mama Sinestra was in the bedroom alone, and that is when she had a chance to do a very nasty deed. I believe she slit a tiny hole in your grandmother's pillow and put a small knotted cord inside. That enchanted cord will gradually grow into a horrible creature that will try to suck your grandmother's soul right out of her body. If it succeeds, and if Mama Sinestra uses her hateful doll, then your grandmother would become—well, like the awful creature that attacked us up at Charley's place."

Johnny felt sick. He imagined his grandmother lurching around as a zombie, her skin pale and clammy, her eyes filmed and blank. "We gotta stop her!" he shouted.

"Easy, Johnny," said Father Higgins. "Roderick, if anybody else had come to me with such a story, I'd—well, I don't know what I'd do. But as you say, we have been through some uncanny times together, so I believe you. What do we have to do?"

"Higgy, I will want you over here tomorrow morning at eight sharp," answered the professor. "Bring with you your priestly bag of tricks—holy water, missal, relics, anything that will offer some protection. You will have to help us deactivate this dire spell. Johnny, you bring the pillow. And Byron, you could stay home and forget the whole thing, but knowing you, I suppose there isn't a prayer of that happening."

"Nope," agreed Fergie with a grin. "Count me in, Prof! Say, is that the way that ol' Mama Sinestra made the zombie that grabbed John? By stickin' somethin' nasty in his beddy-bye pillow?"

Professor Childermass frowned. "Probably not," he said. "You see, a zombie is a body without a soul. It is animated by a spirit, but it has no memory of its former life. That can happen if the soul is stolen away, as I suspect is happening with Johnny's grandmother, but it can also happen if a *voudon* witch doctor calls a spirit into a freshly dead body. Of course, the body must not have been embalmed—even the snazziest witch doctor could do little with a cadaver whose blood has been replaced by formaldehyde! I suspect that the zombie that John and I encountered was merely the unfortunate corpse of this wretched Mr. Jacques Dupont, activated by the abominable Mama Sinestra. Interestingly enough, Mr. Dupont's religion does not permit embalming."

Fergie was grinning wickedly. He had seen some weird and supernatural events in his time, but he was a hard boy to convince, and he reveled in his skepticism. He said, "Yeah, an' maybe Mama Whatserface just hired an actor to clomp around an' scare the two of you silly."

Surprisingly, the professor took this in stride. "Possibly, Byron, but I incline to the more sorcerous explanation. I would have broken the hand of any living man with that tire iron, and I would have killed any normal person when I ran over the creature with my car. The brute showed superhuman strength, just as zombies are supposed to do."

"Maybe it was Gorgeous George the wrestler," said Fergie with a smile. "By the way, you said you had found out about that weirdo drum."

The professor looked startled. "I almost forgot," he admitted. "I guess I'm getting old. Well, Dr. Armitage at Miskatonic U. tells me that classic voodoo drums come in three assorted sizes: There is the largest drum, the *maman* or *grande*; the middle-sized drum, or *seconde*; and the wee little baby drum, or *bébé*. They are all used in magic ceremonies. The *grande* allows the voodoo priest, or *bocor*, to control spirits. The *seconde* guides the spirits so that they will possess certain living people. And the *bébé*, which must be the type that you pounded on, calls up those spirits in the first place. By the way, Byron, do you happen to recall the word you chanted while you were tapping away at the drum?"

Fergie wrinkled his face. "Sure," he said. "I started singin' 'Babaloo,' just like Ricky Ricardo in *I Love Lucy*."

"Yes," agreed the professor in a dry tone. "Well, my unmusical friend, Mr. Ricardo's chant is actually taken from an ancient drum ritual. Dr. Armitage tells me that the word is really *Babaloa* or *Papaloa*, and it is one name for Baron Samedi, a voodoo spirit of great potency who has the ability to possess living people. When he appears, the first thing he does is to summon up power. You may recall how the electric lines went down the moment you screeched out the word. At the time we thought it was just the storm, but now I wonder. In real voodoo ceremonies, huge bonfires provide energy for the spirits. Couldn't electricity work just as well? And you are very, very lucky, Byron. The spirit could have dived right into your body instead of returning to its former dwelling place."

"Where was that?" asked Fergie.

The professor gave him an irritated glance. "Why, in the drum, of course," he said. "Why else do you think Mama Sinestra would be so anxious to get the blasted boom-ba-de-boom back?"

Everything went as the professor planned. Johnny managed to slip into his house without anyone noticing the huge lump that swelled his jacket, and the next morning he tiptoed into his grandparents' room. He took Gramma's pillow from its pillowcase and substituted the one he had brought over from the professor's house. Then he made the bed up again very carefully. He stuffed his grandmother's pillow into an old satchel that he sometimes kept his skates and other sports equipment in and then went downstairs. Gramma was preparing breakfast, and Grampa and Johnny's dad were arguing about whether World War I or World War II was the greatest war of the century. Johnny took his place and ate a tasty breakfast of sausages and buckwheat pancakes. Gramma picked at her own food and muttered that she didn't have much of an appetite. Johnny could see that his dad was worried about her, and he had to admit that Gramma looked ill.

As soon as breakfast ended, Johnny ran up to his room, grabbed the satchel, and headed out the door. He saw Fergie, and the two of them hurried across the street, where the professor swung the door open before they could even knock. "Ah, I see the booty is here," he said, taking the satchel from Johnny. "We've got the pillow and we've got the priest, so let's put the two together and see what happens!"

They went up to the study. Johnny gaped at the transformation that Father Higgins had brought about. The huge desk stood with its top completely bare of papers, books, and the other clutter that the professor always kept there. A white cloth draped the cleared desk, and on the cloth a Bible rested beside a gold crucifix. Father Higgins was in what he called his work clothes, his priestly vestments: the long white robe, or alb, and purple stole. "Roderick, do you suppose we should let these boys stay?" he asked. "This might be ugly, from what you've told me."

"Hey!" protested Fergie at once. "No fair, Father! We were in at the beginning of this, an' we oughta be here for the finish of it!"

Professor Childermass nodded his agreement. "I think so too, Byron. Well, Higgy, tell us what to do."

Briefly, Father Higgins explained that he had consecrated the room as a sort of substitute chapel. He had them pull the pillow out of the satchel and put it on the desk, near the crucifix. Then he led them all in prayer. Professor Childermass and Johnny, who both attended St. Michael's, had no difficulty in following along, but Fergie was a Baptist, and he stumbled over some of the responses. In a kind voice Father Higgins prompted him whenever he had trouble. Then Father Higgins produced a silver container of holy water. He sprinkled this over the pillow—and immediately something strange began to happen.

"Look at that!" shouted Fergie as the pillow began to writhe and pulsate. "It's got some kinda animal in it!"

The pillow did indeed look as if a rabbit or other small creature were trying to find its way out. It heaved and twisted, writhed and swelled. Speaking firmly, Father Higgins commanded the unclean spirit to depart in the name of the Father, the Son, and the Holy Ghost. As Johnny stared with wide eyes, a tiny rip appeared in the seam of the pillow, growing larger and larger with a sound of tearing threads. They all fell back from the desk as feathers began to fly out of the hole. Something that looked slick and wet and gray thrust itself out, and suddenly the pillow ripped itself to shreds in a puff of feathers and down.

Professor Childermass cried out in revulsion. At first Johnny could hardly see for the feathers, but then they settled. Flopping and thrashing about on the desk was a weird form, something like a skinned monkey without a tail. It had a tiny body, a head no larger than an orange, and four long, skinny limbs. It glistened a sick, wet, silvery-gray color, like the slimy belly of a slug. The head showed no eyes or nose, just a pouchy, drooling mouth. The creature mewed and squalled and flapped its useless arms and legs. The sounds it made were horrible, like the bawling of a baby animal in terrible pain. "My God!" exclaimed Professor Childermass. "What is it, Father?"

"Something that does not belong on this earth," responded Father Higgins. "Depart, foul spirit!" And he sprinkled the holy water again.

As the drops spattered it, the creature rose on its two spidery hind legs, screaming and yelping. Wherever the water touched it, its body began to smoke. Then a long, jagged rip appeared in its belly. The body turned inside out, and from it issued a flood of—

Feathers. Wet, gummy, clotted feathers. An incredible quantity gushed out, falling with squishy *plop*s to the floor. Piles of them lay steaming on the desk, filling the room with an ungodly stench. The creature shuddered and collapsed and then was still. Everyone took a step or two forward as the slickly gleaming membrane withered and shriveled like the rubber skin of a leaky old balloon. "Ya did it," crowed Fergie. "Attaboy, Father! Fastest crucifix in the west!" He leaned forward. "Say, Prof, what's this?"

"Don't touch it!" shouted Johnny.

Fergie ignored him. From the mess on the desk he plucked a brown, knotted cord about ten inches long. It dangled with a few wet feathers clinging to it. The professor gingerly took it from him and flung it into the fire. "That, Byron, was the heart of this unholy creature. That cord with its twenty-one secret knots was what Mama Sinestra slipped into Kate Dixon's pillow. Ever since, it has been absorbing life from her, creating this loathsome creature of feathers. Fortunately, Father Higgins stopped it before it had gone very far. Now, Johnny, your grandmother should feel better. At least this horror won't be drawing the life out of her as she sleeps."

"Is—is it all over, then?" gasped Johnny.

The professor looked very angry. "No, my boy, I am

sorry to say that it is not. It is only beginning. Next we have to locate that foul doll, and then we have to do the same for Charley, and that may be the hardest thing we will ever have to do."

"Any ideas on where the doll of Johnny's granma is, Prof?" asked Fergie eagerly.

The professor nodded. "Yes, Byron, I have an idea or two, but this time you cannot tag along." He raised his hand to shut off Fergie's protest. "No use, Byron. I have already discussed this with Father Higgins, and he agrees with me. The place where we have to go next is—well, even in ordinary times it would be terrifying. And with Mama Sinestra around it may be deadly. So no, you may not come with us."

To Johnny's surprise, Fergie said, "Okay, Prof, if you put your foot down, then so be it—but you know how I hate to miss a party!"

The relief Johnny felt was very short-lived. A few minutes later, as he and Fergie left the professor's house, Fergie turned to him with a grin. "We're on stakeout, partner," he said.

"Huh?" asked Johnny.

Fergie winked. "The prof and Father Higgins may think they can ditch us, but all we gotta do is keep a watch on the house. I'll get my folks t' let me stay over, an' we won't let 'em get away from us. When those two close in for the arrest in the case of the killer doll, deputies Johnny Dixon an' Fergie Ferguson are gonna be right there with them!"

Johnny's stomach churned as he remembered the feather monster and what the professor said were even worse things, but already he knew he was a goner. If Fergie wanted them in on the case, then he had to go along. He only hoped they would get out of the adventure alive.

CHAPTER NINE

Nothing more happened that day, nor the next one. Gramma had perked up quite a bit, though, and Major Dixon began to look more cheerful. He and Johnny had a couple of chats about what each had been doing over the past several months. Major Dixon said that regardless of Johnny's decision, he and Johnny would vacation together next summer, and they spent some time dreaming up places they could go.

Meanwhile, Johnny kept an eye open for any sign of activity at the professor's house, but he saw nothing out of the ordinary. Professor Childermass was at home: Johnny saw him come out to collect his morning paper on both Saturday and Sunday, and his maroon Pontiac stayed parked at the curb in front of his house. And

Johnny saw no sign of Father Higgins' big Oldsmobile.

Fergie spent both Friday and Saturday nights. During the day he and Johnny practiced throwing and catching a football in front of Johnny's house. It gave them the opportunity of keeping the professor's house under observation without seeming to spy on it. Johnny was lousy at sports. He was not well coordinated, so many boys didn't even want to play catch with him. But Fergie didn't mind, and since Fillmore Street was always very quiet, they could stand right out in the street and pass the football back and forth.

Their stakeout paid off Sunday evening. Like most boys their age, Johnny and Fergie had a tendency to put off homework until the last minute. Fergie had a big test in Latin coming up, and he was not very good at it. Johnny, whose average in Latin had never fallen below an A, offered to help him review, so the two spent a couple of hours that afternoon running through noun declensions. At about eight P.M. Fergie heard a car outside and got up to look out the window. "It's Higgy," he said in an excited voice. "C'mon, John baby. It's time to fish or cut bait!"

Johnny didn't know exactly what that meant, but he closed his book, grabbed his jacket, and followed Fergie. His dad and Grampa were deep in a game of checkers, and Gramma was in the kitchen humming to herself. Johnny casually waved to his grandfather, knowing that the old man would think he was just walking Fergie partway home. Grampa barely nodded, and then with a triumphant grin he made a double jump on the checkerboard.

The two boys walked onto the porch just in time to see the professor's door close as Father Higgins went into the house. "I bet they're gettin' ready to go right now," said Fergie. "What a break!"

"What are we gonna do?" asked Johnny, feeling cross. "Sneak into the house and spy on them?"

"Nope," said Fergie in a smug tone. "We're gonna stow away. C'mon, Dixon, we better move fast!"

They loped across the street. Hardly anyone in Duston Heights ever locked his car, so when Fergie tried the back door of the Oldsmobile, Johnny was not surprised that it clicked open. Fergie climbed inside and hunched down on the floor behind the front seat. "C'mon," he whispered. "An' close the door carefully."

Feeling like a fool, Johnny got onto the backseat floor and pulled the door closed without making much noise. "Now what?" whispered Johnny.

"Now we wait, John baby. If they're goin' anywhere, they'll be out in a few minutes. An' if we just sit tight and quiet, they'll haul us along with them!"

Fergie's cocksure attitude irritated Johnny. "What if Professor Childermass drives *his* car, smart guy?" he asked.

Fergie snickered. "Not a chance. You know what a rotten driver he is, an' so does Higgy. Nope, if they're goin' anywhere, it'll be in this car, so all we gotta do is keep from bein' seen. I got it all—Shh!"

The professor's front door opened, and two figures emerged. They came toward the car, and Johnny scrunched down, making himself as small as he could. Sure enough, in a second the passenger-side front door opened and someone got in, making the car settle a little on its springs, and a moment later the driver slid behind the wheel. "You have everything you need, don't you?" asked the professor's raspy, crabby voice.

"For the last time, yes, yes, and yes," said Father Higgins peevishly. The engine started, and as the car pulled away from the curb the priest said, "Rod, I hope you know what you are doing. It seems like a long shot to me."

The professor snorted. "Long shot, my foot! Look, Higgy, all my research shows that the *voudon* doll gains power if it is kept in a place of death until it is ready to be used. Well, what places of death do we have around here? I'll tell you: the funeral parlors and the cemeteries. Now, it doesn't seem likely that Mama Sinestra has taken up residence at any of our local mortuaries, so that leaves the cemeteries—where the power of Baron Samedi, Lord of the Dead, is at its greatest. That is why I asked you to find out if anything suspicious had been noted in or around our local boneyards."

The car was moving steadily now. "And that ridiculous report about a bear prowling through Rest Haven Cemetery is your so-called lead?"

Fergie tapped Johnny's knee in an I-told-you-so kind of way. Professor Childermass sighed deeply. "That was no bear, as you well know. Think, Higgy! The woman said she saw a black shape, squat and heavy and shuffling. Who fits that description?"

"Mama Sinestra," agreed Father Higgins, his reluctance evident in his voice.

"Exactly. And isn't Rest Haven a logical place? I mean, the Dixon family *does* have relatives buried there, and that is where Henry and Kate have their plots."

"So do half the Catholics in town," said Father Higgins. "Anyway, we'll soon know, because here we are. I got the key to the gates from the groundskeeper. Should we unlock them and drive in?"

"Heavens, no," replied the professor. "You were in the army long enough to know the value of surprise. We'll park at the curb and then go inside on foot. Since the doll needs constant attention until the charm is exactly right, Mama Sinestra must have settled in someplace that gives her protection from the elements. That means a mausoleum, and there are only a half dozen or so. We'll check them out one by one until we find the old hag, and then give her holy hopping what for!"

Father Higgins parked beneath a streetlight. Johnny squinched himself into as tight a ball as possible, and he could see that Fergie was doing the same. They need not have worried, because both Professor Childermass and Father Higgins were far too excited and preoccupied to notice them as the two men slammed the car doors shut and walked away. A few seconds later Fergie said, "Peek out your window, Dixon, and see if the coast is clear."

Cautiously, Johnny raised himself enough to peer out. He could see the black wrought-iron fence that ran around the cemetery. It was about ten feet tall, and every tenth rail was a foot again taller than that, with a decorative spear-tip end on it. Through the rails of the fence, Johnny could just make out the glimmering white oblongs of marble headstones in the darkness. He saw no sign of the two men. "They must've gone in," he said.

"Let's go." Fergie and Johnny crept out of the car and walked to the front gates of the cemetery. Fortunately, Father Higgins had not locked these behind him, and the boys slipped through, though the old hinges did groan a rusty protest. "Rats," muttered Fergie. "I shoulda thought to bring a flashlight. Why aren't there any lights in this place?"

"Who'd need them?" asked Johnny. He felt uneasy and excited, as if something awe inspiring but terrible might happen at any second. He gazed around, but at first all he could see was the vague blur of headstones. Only a little stray light from the streetlamps penetrated this far into the graveyard. Then Johnny caught sight of a moving gleam just over the crest of a hill. He croaked, "Hey—there's a light, over that way." He and Fergie hurried up the hill, and as soon as they got to the top, they spotted the shapes of two men walking slowly among the tombstones.

One of the men had a flashlight, and the boys followed its wavering yellow beam at a respectful distance. Walking was difficult because Rest Haven was an old cemetery, and the gravestones were crowded together. Johnny had served as an altar boy for St. Michael's, and he had assisted Father Higgins at four or five funerals here, so he knew his way around. He and Fergie drew closer to the light until they were just near enough to hear the thin voices of Father Higgins and the professor. Right now the professor sounded testy: "Well, of course I didn't expect to find it first crack off the bat! Come on, Higgy, where's the next one?"

"Don't call me Higgy, Rod. You know I hate that."

"And I hate being called Rod, Higgy. Come on—the faster you tell me where the next mausoleum is, the faster we'll be out of here."

"The Famagusta family mausoleum," muttered Father Higgins. "Just over this way. Don't fall over the headstones!"

The two men came up to a big marble mausoleum that was almost the size of a small house and designed as a miniature Greek temple. Four Corinthian columns supported the rectangular entablature beneath the pediment, which was triangular. A small stone angel guarded each corner of the triangle. The two on either side bore swords, and the one on the peak was stretching her arms high over her head, carrying a wreath. Carved into the marble of the pediment was the single word FAMAGUSTA. Johnny knew all these details from memory, because it was far too dark to see them right now. He fleetingly wondered if the dead people inside the fancy mausoleum were related to the caretaker of St. Michael's. If so, the family had fallen on hard times, because Mr. Famagusta was as poor as a church mouse.

Then Johnny heard Father Higgins gasp. "Look at this!" he said. "Why, this door has been tampered with—someone sawed the padlock off!"

"As I predicted," replied the professor dryly, inspecting the bar and the heavy bronze doors. "Now, if you have quite finished alerting whoever is inside to our presence, let's get on with it— *Hah!*"

The professor must have yanked the metal door open hard, because it clanged with a noise that made Johnny jump a mile. "Good God, Roderick!" shouted the priest, but his voice sounded more irritated than alarmed. "A little more of that, and you'll awaken these Famagustas and all their neighbors!"

"Sorry," muttered the professor. "Nobody home, it seems, but just take a look inside here—there are some empty tins of canned heat, and there are some worn old blankets in the corner. Someone has been sleeping in this mausoleum—sleeping temporarily, I mean, not eternally!"

Fergie squirmed beside Johnny. "I can't see a thing," he complained. "C'mon, Dixon, let's circle around."

The two boys picked their way cautiously until they could gaze in through the open door. Johnny felt the hair prickling on his neck and arms at the eerie sight. Inside the mausoleum coffins lay on shelves. Father Higgins stood with his back to a whole wall of them, shining his flashlight down so that the coffins were just indistinct shadowy forms. The professor knelt on the floor, rummaging through a pile of tattered brown Army surplus blankets. "Aha!" they heard him cry. He held up something small and blue. "Father Higgins, you may offer your sincere apologies anytime you wish. Here it is!"

Fergie made a squeaking, stifled noise, and Johnny looked at him. He could barely see Fergie's face in the dark, but his friend seemed terrified as he stared with wide eyes into the mausoleum. Johnny looked back.

Someone was stirring in the darkness behind Father Higgins. Someone or something. One of the coffins behind the priest swung open slowly and silently. And then the body inside it sat up!

"Run!" screamed Johnny at the top of his lungs. "Professor, Father, run! *There's a zombie behind you!*"

CHAPTER TEN

Both Father Higgins and Professor Childermass jumped. Then Father Higgins swung around and brought his flashlight beam up. Cold horror clutched Johnny's heart. Just getting to his feet was the zombie, his slack, lifeless face baleful and appalling. Father Higgins reacted very quickly: He rushed the zombie and shoved his chest, hard. "Run!" he shouted as the zombie toppled backward, landing half in and half out of the coffin.

Professor Childermass scurried out the door, with Father Higgins close behind him. The priest slammed the bronze doors closed with a clamor that sent echoes clattering back and forth across the cemetery. "Quick!" he yelled. "Pull the bar down!"

A heavy horizontal bar held the doors closed. It fit

into a frame, and normally a padlock hung in a hole drilled through both bar and frame. The padlock had been sawn off, but the bar would hold the doors closed—anyone inside the tomb would be trapped there. Professor Childermass drove the bar down with a loud *clang* as Father Higgins turned his flashlight toward the boys. "Johnny! Fergie!" he yelled. "Is that you?"

Fergie and Johnny had crouched low behind a long headstone. Both stood up, and immediately the priest's flashlight beam shone on them. "Yeah," yelled Fergie. "An' a good thing for you too! That creep nearly had ya!" He bolted around the headstone and ran over to the two men, with Johnny following close on his heels.

"How on earth did you two get here?" demanded an annoyed Professor Childermass. "Byron, Johnny, I am deeply disappointed in—"

Crash! The monster inside the tomb smashed against the bronze doors. Father Higgins shone his light there and cried out in alarm. Johnny felt sick. With a single blow, the creature had forced the doors open enough for its pale, dead hand to come over the top edge. The fingers clutched at the bronze door and pressed hard, and the heavy door actually began to *bend*. The zombie was forcing its way out!

"We have what we came for—let's go!" shouted Father Higgins. "Boys, my car is—"

"Yeah, we know," replied Fergie. "C'mon."

Father Higgins took the lead with his flashlight, and Professor Childermass brought up the rear. With the aid of the light, they stuck to the paths between the graves and made good time, but before they reached the front gates of the cemetery, they all heard an unholy clatter of metal. The zombie must have wrenched the doors right off their hinges, and the creature was behind them, somewhere in the darkness. Johnny could picture him lumbering blindly along between the graves, his dead hands thrust out to grab a victim—

"Quick!" yelled the priest. They had arrived at the cemetery gate. Father Higgins held it open while the other three dashed out, and then he slammed and locked it. They piled into the Oldsmobile, and Father Higgins revved the motor before the car leaped away from the curb with a screech of tires. They were all gasping for breath.

Johnny said to Fergie, "Now—now—do you—believe me about the—the zombie?"

Fergie, who was not quite so winded, sounded as if he were sneering: "Maybe, John baby. I'll admit I was scared for a minute, but that might have been just a crazy old guy. They say that lunatics have superhuman strength sometimes, ya know!"

Professor Childermass growled, "That was no lunatic. That was the late Mr. Jacques Dupont. Blast it all! I should have realized that Mama Sinestra would have a watchdog guard her precious little toy. But we have the doll, and there's not a moment to lose. Now I want to consult my books as we deal with this evil little image. Higgy, let's head back to my place."

On the way the professor mildly scolded Johnny and Fergie for sneaking along on the expedition, but without much real anger. The old man knew that Fergie had been right: Without Johnny's shouted warning, both Father Higgins and he would have fallen victim to the zombie's incredible strength. In a few minutes the car stopped in front of the professor's house, and they all climbed out. Johnny looked at the luminous hands of his watch and was astonished to see that only forty minutes had gone by since he and Fergie had slipped into the car. It seemed much longer.

Once again they all gathered in the professor's study, where Professor Childermass laid the doll on the cloth-covered desk. "Now," he said, "I am afraid that your holy water and missal won't work here, Higgy. We have to *unmake* the doll—take it apart, doing no damage to the fabric at all if we can help it. It may not be at full power, but any injury we cause the doll might rebound on poor Kate Dixon."

Johnny looked at the horrible doll with a fascinated curiosity. It had changed somehow since his first glimpse of it. It still wore the same blue gingham dress and white apron, but the face had more form now. Where it had once been featureless, the cloth had begun to pucker and wrinkle. One wrinkle suggested a mouth, two little dimples were in the right place for eyes, and between them a nose had begun to form. The face looked like a very blurry snapshot of his grandmother. He shivered, grateful that the spell had not reached its completion. He suspected that if it had, the doll would have been a dead ringer for Gramma.

The professor fussed with the seams of the doll. At last he smiled grimly as he peered at the doll's hand. "Here is the knot that holds the thread," he muttered, "but hang it all, Mama S. has left us no slack. I don't want to cut the knot, although we might try burning it in two—fire is said to purify evil." He fetched a needle, which he stuck through the eraser of a pencil. Then he used his tacky cigarette lighter, which was in the shape of a knight in armor, to heat the point of the needle red-hot. With the light touch of a surgeon, the professor barely grazed the thread with the needle tip. A little wisp of smoke curled up, and the thread parted. "There!" said Professor Childermass with an air of satisfaction. "Now we can unmake the thing."

With infinite care, he used the point of a second, cool needle to take out the stitches that held the doll together. He opened it up and took from inside a wad of cotton, with about a dozen white hairs wound around it. He plucked the cotton away and made sure he counted the hairs into a separate pile. When he finished, he muttered, "Thirteen! We might have guessed, eh? Now, Higgy, just to be safe, bless this pile of cloth and cotton and hair, and then we'll burn it."

"Burn it?" yelped Johnny in dismay. "But won't that—"

"No," said the professor firmly. "I have unmade the doll, and now it is harmless. To take off any lingering spell, Father Higgins will do his bit, and then the parts of the doll will be just powerless pieces of cloth, wads of cotton, and strands of hair. So go ahead, Father Higgins, and do your blessedest!"

The priest performed a brief ritual of blessing, and then they ceremonially burned the cloth, cotton, and hair. Johnny ran home right away, and he found Gramma looking well but a little puzzled. "Hi," he said as he came in.

"Oh, Johnny," she replied. "I was just goin' to the upstairs bathroom. Is that where the Bactine is, do you know?"

When anything surprised Johnny, he stammered. "Uh, s-sure. It's in th-the m-medicine cabinet. Why?"

Gramma held up her right forefinger. It had a big blister on it, just on the outside of the joint. "Beats the life out o' me how I did it, but somehow or other I musta burned the dickens out o' my finger. Didn't even notice it until just a few minutes ago, and then this big ugly thing popped up. But I'll bandage it up, and it'll be better tomorrow."

Later that night, Johnny lay in his bed and wondered at the weird magic of the doll. The professor had been right—the blister on Gramma's finger was at the same place where he had burned through the thread holding the doll together. He shivered, wondering what terrible thing would have happened to Gramma if someone had just cut the thread without taking the time to unmake the doll. It was an awful notion to contemplate, and he fell asleep only with difficulty that Sunday night.

Johnny expected that Professor Childermass would go immediately to New Hampshire to save Dr. Coote, but he was mistaken. The professor explained somberly that he could not use the same methods that had worked with Johnny's grandmother. "We are fighting two different attacks," explained the old man. "First, Mama Sinestra must have made a doll with some of Charley's hair inside it. I checked, and Charley grew ill the morning after the new moon, just when such a doll would have gained full power. That is what landed him in the hospital. Since that doll is finished, Mama Sinestra could use it at any moment to kill our friend."

Johnny swallowed hard. "What else are we fighting?" he asked.

The professor grimaced. "After Charley was hospitalized, the old hag slipped into his room and concealed a knotted cord in his pillow. As the cord grew in power, our friend's mind grew weaker. Now he is in a coma, and that means that the evil creature in his pillow has done its work. So Charley is in much greater danger than your grandmother was. We could splatter the pillow monster with holy water. That might even kill the creature. But since it has already absorbed Charley's mind, he would never come out of his coma. I have to learn how to deactivate the monster before I attempt to deal with it. However, in an odd way I believe that Charley is safe."

"Professor," asked Johnny, "what do you mean, *safe?* He's lying there helpless—"

Professor Childermass raised a finger. "Ah, but he is still alive," he said. "I have been following the events in St. Ives in the newspapers, Johnny, and they are very interesting. General LeGrande, the dictator, is holed up in his palace. The peasants—the ordinary people of the island—are revolting against his corrupt rule. And for the first time, they are winning battles. Do you see what that means?"

"No," said Johnny, knowing that the professor would tell him.

"Well, it means that without the drum, the LeGrande family has lost its grim hold over the island. The only person who knows where the drum is hidden is Charley. Mama Sinestra cannot be sure who has the drum— maybe you, maybe I, maybe Charley—and since she can't take a chance on killing the one person who *might* lead her to the drum, she'd never dare do Charley in."

"What if she gets the drum back?" asked Johnny.

The professor shook his head. "Then God help all of us. We have to prevent that at all costs."

And that was all he would say for the time being. Days passed without Mama Sinestra showing up again. The newspaper made a big row about the "vandalism" at Rest Haven Cemetery. According to the story, someone had dumped the bones of one Rafael Famagusta (1845–1907) out of his coffin and had used a truck to yank the bronze doors off the mausoleum. The paper called for stricter vigilance.

Johnny, Father Higgins, the professor, and Fergie were all vigilant enough, but no one saw the slightest sign of the old sorceress. "We got her on the run," said Fergie, though the others were not so sure. Meanwhile, the professor continued his research, and by mid-December, he thought he had found a way to deal with Charley's problem. They all met again in the professor's study, which had reverted to its ordinary messy condition. The professor had been in touch with Todd Lamort, who reported that Dr. Coote still lay unconscious. Professor Childermass proposed that he, Fergie, and Johnny go up to Portsmouth to deal with the hex on Dr. Coote. Meanwhile, Father Higgins would live in the professor's house and keep a watch on the Dixons across the street—just to make sure that Mama Sinestra didn't try any more tricks.

"I think having a priest nearby would give her second thoughts," the professor finished. "And I believe that the boys and I can handle whatever horror we find in Portsmouth. I wouldn't even take the two of you, mind, but I have a rotten feeling you'd sneak along anyway."

"Now, Prof," said Fergie with a broad, innocent grin, "whatever makes you say that?"

Professor Childermass did not smile. "If you go, Byron, you will consider yourself under my orders. You will do what I say, and if I don't say it, you won't do it. Is that clear?"

For once, Fergie's smart-alecky manner disappeared. "Sure," he said. "You got my word on it, Prof."

"Gentlemen," the professor said, "I want you both to bear in mind one thing. This is a matter of life and death. Your lives. And, God forbid, your deaths!"

CHAPTER ELEVEN

The last day of school before the new year would be Friday, December 17, and as the Christmas vacation drew closer, Johnny grew more and more nervous and troubled. Part of his worry, of course, had to do with the trip he, Fergie, and the professor were taking to Portsmouth on the first Saturday of the Christmas break. Johnny was all too aware of the danger that might lurk. The other part of his worry came from Major Dixon's approaching departure and Johnny's decision about whether he wanted to stay in Duston Heights or move with his father to Atlanta. It was a tough choice, and Johnny felt torn by it. The last week he had gone to St. Michael's Church every afternoon to pray for guidance, but he realized that in the end he alone would have to choose.

He had tried to talk the matter over with the professor, but the old man had his own deep worries, as did Father Higgins. Fergie was not much help either. When Johnny brought the matter up, Fergie made a face. "Aw, Dixon, you know you belong in Duston Heights," he said. "Who else can teach you to play baseball, an' who else can keep me humble by beatin' me at chess?"

But that was not enough for Johnny, even though he had to admit he would miss Fergie terribly. Fergie had become the very best friend he had ever had. Even so, Johnny felt that he needed unbiased advice, not Fergie's wisecracks. With the professor, Father Higgins, and Fergie unable or unwilling to advise him, Johnny became more and more upset. In a way it was almost a relief when Saturday morning came and he once again got into the professor's maroon Pontiac for the drive north. Three or four snowstorms had covered Duston Heights with a crusted layer of snow. The streets were clear, though, and the professor had put snow tires on his car, so they were ready for any weather. Professor Childermass stopped in Cranbrook, the snooty section of Duston Heights, where Fergie lived. Fergie came out lugging his plaid suitcase, and he clambered into the backseat of the car next to Johnny. Fergie's dad, a mild-looking, balding man who sold Bibles, shoes, and kitchenware door to door, came out to wave good-bye, and Fergie gave his father a jaunty salute. Then the three of them sped away on their mission.

As they drove to Portsmouth, the professor explained what he intended to do. The danger, he said, was that the cord that Mama Sinestra must have placed in Dr. Coote's pillow had turned into a fully developed monster that had fed off Dr. Coote's conscious mind, his soul, which the *voudon* priests called the *gros bon ange*. What kept Dr. Coote alive was the spirit of life itself, or the *ti bon ange*. If the creature that Mama Sinestra created were simply destroyed, then Dr. Coote's soul would not be able to return to the old man's body, and he would exist like a vegetable for the rest of his life.

So the professor could not simply splash the feathery horror with holy water, as Father Higgins had done with the one from Gramma's pillow. Instead, he would have to perform a certain ritual that would separate the creature from Dr. Coote's psyche. That would be dangerous, because without a human mind to occupy and control it, the beast would be free to attack anyone it pleased. If he completed the ritual correctly, however, the professor would hold the uncanny creature captive inside a spell of his own. The professor had brought along with him a black leather valise with crumbling corners and rusty hinges, something like a doctor's bag. Inside were some magical implements that he had borrowed from his friend at Miskatonic University, which he hoped would help him set Dr. Coote free of the awful enchantment.

Fergie listened as the professor talked, and then he said, "Swell, Prof. So what do me an' Johnny do? Stand guard with our holy-water sprinklers an' douse the critter if it acts up?"

"No," Professor Childermass said sternly. "I definitely do *not* want that. Byron, you and Johnny will have to stand guard, all right—but *outside* the door of the hospital room. I will have to use all my concentration to make sure I can control this—this whirlamadoodle from the infernal regions. If I have to worry about you, Johnny, and Charley all at once, then I may very well become distracted, and that would be fatal for everyone."

"Aw, Prof," objected Fergie. "You know we can take care of ourselves."

Professor Childermass set his mouth in a stubborn line. He clammed up, but as he drove, he thought about the problem. He had told the boys only half of his motives for taking them along. It was true that the three of them had shared some wild adventures, and equally true that he valued their companionship and moral support. However, it was also true that he was afraid to leave them in Duston Heights.

He had not told anyone else, but the professor had called the police in Duston Heights, Portsmouth, and Durham. He had described Mama Sinestra to them and had suggested that she was a deranged and dangerous character. All had promised to keep an eye out for her, but so far she had not been seen. As long as he did not know where Mama Sinestra was, the professor preferred having Johnny and Fergie with him—at least, he thought, she wouldn't get a crack at them in Duston Heights while he was prancing around like some witch doctor in Portsmouth. However, he had no intention of exposing Fergie and Johnny to the dangerous possibility of the ritual's going wrong, so he pondered about what he could do to insure that the boys were safe.

He still had not solved the problem when he drove the Pontiac into the parking lot of Mercy Hospital. He picked his black bag up from the passenger seat and then groaned as they all stepped out of the car into the slush. "Look at this," he said, his voice angry. "These Portsmouth people don't even scrape out the parking lots. They just throw rock salt all over everything to get rid of the snow. Disgraceful!"

"What's wrong with that, Prof?" asked Fergie. "I mean, the salt melts the snow anyway, right?"

Professor Childermass glared at Byron. "Oh, yes, indeedy, it melts the snow. And when a car goes rolling through this slush and mush, the salt flies up against the frame. And then what happens, my fine feathered friend?"

"Uh—you get a car that tastes like a pretzel?" teased Fergie, who knew the answer very well.

"No!" exploded the professor. "You get rust, rust, rust! Also known as ferrous oxide! And what does rust do to a car? It destroys it! All because these cheapo New Hampshirites are too tightfisted to invest in a couple of road scrapers! If I had them here right now, I'd—"

"Professor," pleaded Johnny, "we have to be quiet in the hospital!"

Professor Childermass noticed then for the first time that they had walked into the lobby of the hospital, where people sitting in chairs were looking at him curiously. He glared back with defiance. "If any of you people work for the government department that salts the streets here," he said in a quiet but furious voice, "you should be ashamed of yourselves!" Then he stalked over to the nurses' station and signed himself and the boys in as visitors.

They went upstairs, with Fergie wondering aloud where they did amputations and autopsies. Johnny elbowed him in the ribs. "Be quiet, won'tcha?" he muttered. "You're gonna make them throw us out!"

Fergie piped down, though he was still grinning mischievously. When they opened the door of Dr. Coote's room, Todd Lamort, who was sitting in a chair next to the bed, glanced up from the book he had been reading. Dr. Coote looked awful. He had lost weight, and his usually fluffy white hair was pasted against his head. His eyes were closed and his wide mouth was slightly open. Strips of white adhesive tape held a tube in place inside his left nostril. He wore striped pajamas, and his long, bony arms lay on top of the blanket, the knotted old hands half clenched. Johnny had to glance away. Dr. Coote looked like a dying man.

"Hello," whispered Todd Lamort. "I didn't know you were coming."

"It's kind of a spur-of-the-moment visit," replied Professor Childermass, setting his black bag down at the foot of the hospital bed. "How has he been?"

Lamort shook his head sadly. "Every once in a while he will mutter and groan, but he doesn't recognize anyone, and he won't talk to me, no matter how hard I try to get him to speak."

"Hm," said Professor Childermass. "I hate to see poor Charley in this dreadful state. Have you had any more trouble at his house?"

"No," replied Lamort. "I've been staying in the guest room, because that drippy toilet keeps me awake. No one has tried to break in, and everything has been very quiet."

The professor nodded. "It's kind of you to stay there," he said. "And to visit Dr. Coote. I know he would want to thank you if he could."

Lamort gave an embarrassed sort of smile. "Well, it's the least I could do," he murmured. He stretched and yawned. "I think I will leave now that you are here. I have one last examination on Monday before Christmas, and I need to study. Is there anything I can do?"

"No, thank you," said Professor Childermass. Then he snapped his fingers. "Or rather, yes, now that I think about it. How about taking Johnny and Byron with you? I want to stay and visit with my old friend, but there's nothing they can do here. At least at Dr. Coote's house they might play chess, or read books from his collection of occult classics."

"Sure," said Lamort. "If they don't mind riding in my beat-up old Ford, I'd be glad to take them."

So Johnny and Fergie went with Todd Lamort, leaving the professor in Dr. Coote's room. To tell the truth, Johnny felt nothing but relief. Dr. Coote looked so terrible that he hated to be there—even though he felt guilty about deserting the old man. Fergie seemed irritated at missing the ritual, though he chatted with Lamort. "Ya French Canadian?" he asked as they slopped across the slushy parking lot.

"No," Lamort said. "I have French ancestors, though. What made you think I was French Canadian?"

"Your name," Fergie said. "We got lotsa Canucks in Duston Heights, an' I thought maybe they were here too."

"Sorry to disappoint you," said Lamort with a smile. They came to an old black 1947 Ford, its paint dull and rusty spots showing on its fenders. The upholstery in the car must have been full of holes, because Lamort had thrown brown Army blankets over both the front and back seats. The passenger side of the front seat held some papers and maps, so Fergie and Johnny got into the back. Lamort got the balky engine started after three or four tries, and they clattered out of the lot.

"I want to make a stop before we go to Dr. Coote's house," said Lamort. "It isn't far out of the way."

They drove north toward Durham as Lamort apologized that the car heater wasn't working. They passed the University of New Hampshire campus and drove into the countryside. Durham is just a small village except for the university, and so they were soon away from civilization. Lamort took a rutted side road, and before long a dilapidated old two-story farmhouse came into view. The barn had collapsed years ago and was hardly more than a jumble of ancient boards, frosted with snow. The house itself was bare of paint, and the walls looked ready to tumble down, but someone was inside, because a drift of smoke came from one of the two chimneys. "You might as well come in and get warmed up," he said. "I'll be just a few minutes."

With the heater out of commission the Ford was frigid, so Johnny and Fergie gladly clambered out of the car. Lamort led them around to the back of the house. They walked into a warm kitchen, where an old black wood-burning stove crackled and snapped. A coffeepot perked on the stove. Lamort closed the door behind Johnny and Fergie.

"*Grand-mère!*" he called.

Flowered curtains hung over a doorway. A hand reached out and parted them, and an old woman came into the kitchen. She had long, straggly, gray hair, eyes that were squinched into slits by pouches of fat, and a broad, evil mouth. Johnny and Fergie yelled simultaneously. Todd Lamort's hands clamped onto their shoulders, keeping them from running.

"Boys," purred Lamort, "I'd like you to meet my grandmother. You can call her Mama Sinestra!"

CHAPTER TWELVE

If anyone had looked into Room 315 of Mercy Hospital that morning, he would have thought that a crazy man had come to see Dr. Coote. Professor Childermass had unpacked his black case and had made his preparations. Seven candles burned in the room: two white ones on tables at the head of Dr. Coote's bed, two red ones on the floor at the bed's foot, two blue ones between the red ones, and between the blue candles a single, sinister black one. Beside one of the white candles rested a silver holy-water sprinkler. The professor had also taken out three small cloth bags full of dyed cornmeal. One bag held red cornmeal, one held black, and the third held yellow. Working carefully, the professor dribbled little lines of the powdery substance on the floor, making what the voodoo priests called a *vévé*, a mystical drawing that produced strong magic. His friend at Miskatonic University had given him a number of designs that supposedly harnessed good magical forces. The professor repeatedly consulted a drawing of one of these designs as he shaped the lines of cornmeal into a pattern that involved a Valentine heart, intersecting lines with feathery twiglike markings on their ends, and a central circle with an eye in it. Then the professor took several bright-red silk neckerchiefs from the bag. He tied one of these around his head and knotted others together to loop around his middle like a sash.

That done, he paused, bowed his head, and said several prayers, asking for strength, courage, and the assistance of heavenly powers. Then he faced the moment he dreaded. The professor went to the bed, slipped the pillow from beneath Dr. Coote's head, and placed it in the center of the *vévé* he had drawn. He used his pocketknife to slit the pillow open, and he glanced fearfully inside. Sure enough, although the pillow still had the texture of a bag filled with feathers, he could see something revolting and frightening. It looked like a coiled reptile with scaly, sickly-gray skin. The professor's heart pounded as he gently shook the thing from its nest inside the pillow. Then he stepped back.

For a moment the creature simply lay motionless, a confusing, tightly coiled bundle of arms, legs, and scales. It was a pale, slimy gray-white, and though it had felt soft, the professor could see the outlines of bones through its scaly skin. Slowly, ever so slowly, the incredible thing began to move. First a limb straightened out, revealing itself to be a leg, ending in a grotesque foot with long toes and sharp claws. It looked like a bird's foot, except that it had four forward-facing toes and a viciously curved short claw back where the heel should be. Then the arms unclasped. The being pushed itself to a standing position, and as it did, it grew. It was unbelievably skinny, but it was taller than the professor when at last it stood upright. The legs and arms were little more than stems, with knotted knees and elbows. The belly was shrunken, the rib cage hanging over it like the lip of a cavern. The terrible face had snakelike yellow-green eyes with slits for pupils, a hooked nose, and a thin, wide, sneering mouth. A tuft of white feathers on the crown of the head waved as it slowly wagged its round head from side to side on a curving, skinny neck. As the professor watched in sick fascination, the monster gasped for breath, hissing quietly. It started to step toward him, menacingly, but when its clawed toes were over the outline of the heart, it stopped and backed up a pace. It glared at him with hatred.

Professor Childermass felt cold sweat creeping over his face. His heart was thudding like mad, and his mind shrieked for him to run away from this stretched-out monstrosity. Yet he forced himself to smile. "No, no," he said softly. "You are held in check by magic stronger than you are. *You* can't get to *me*—but, my friend, *I* am going to settle *your* hash right now!"

He pulled from his pocket a brown knotted cord, stiff with beeswax. The creature hissed again when it saw what he held. It clawed at the air as if it wished to attack him. "Now, then," said Professor Childermass grimly, "here we go. And may I say first that you deserve this for having the audacity to take on the twisted likeness of my poor friend." Then the professor chanted something in French, which he spoke fluently, and the monster's eyes blazed its defiant malice. "As you are tied to the soul of Dr. Charles Coote," finished the professor, "this cord binds your evil power to you. In the names of all the holy saints, of the blessed Virgin Mary, and of the Father, the Son, and the Holy Ghost, I conjure you to release your hold on this man's soul. Behold, I undo the power that gives you shape and form and strength!" He untied one of the twenty-one knots of his cord, holding it so the creature could see.

It moaned softly and staggered. The spell was working! With grim satisfaction, the professor said the last part of his spell again and then untied another knot, and then another one. Each time, the creature reeled as if in pain, and before he untied each knot, the professor repeated his conjuration. He tried to sound bold and confident, but he grew more and more alarmed. He knew that each knot he untied hurt the creature more. If he could torment it to the point of releasing its hold on Charles Coote's soul, the cord and the *vévé* would have no more power to hold the monster, and it would be free to attack him. On the other hand, if it stubbornly refused to yield its grip on Dr. Coote until the professor undid the last knot, then the evil creature would die. It would die— and take Dr. Coote's soul with it, leaving him bedridden for the rest of his life. Professor Childermass was fighting a savage war of wills, and gambling that he could force the monster to give in before he had to untie that very last knot.

Fifteen knots remained, then twelve, then seven. Now Professor Childermass' hands were shaking with strain. His eyes stung as sweat rolled into them, and his voice kept piping high with dread. But he continued relentlessly. The beastly creature had dropped to crouch on all fours, its hate-filled eyes glaring at the professor as it gasped for air and hissed its anger. The seventh knot was undone! With a sinking heart, Professor Childermass repeated his command, and began to untie the sixth—

And the creature collapsed! The candles burned a sickly blue for a moment, then went out. Curls of smoke rose from the extinguished wicks. The professor groaned, horrified. Had he killed his friend? Had he—

"Roderick?" asked a weak voice. "My God, is it Roderick?"

Professor Childermass shouted in joy. Dr. Coote was sitting up in bed, trembling, his voice weak, his eyes wide and wild, but he was awake. Then another sound, a horrible mindless growl, stopped the professor's rejoicing and brought his heart into his mouth. The pillow thing had risen into a crouch again, and its mad, empty eyes blazed. Now that it no longer possessed a human soul, it was free to ignore all the professor's magical restraints. With a savage roar it leaped—and before the professor could reach for the holy-water sprinkler, it slammed into his chest, knocking him back. His head banged painfully against the wall, and his glasses flew off. The horrible creature's talons closed on the professor's throat, and the mouth split open to reveal hundreds of needle-sharp teeth.

The professor ducked just in time, and the teeth clicked on air. "Help!" shouted the professor as he sank to the floor. The monster weighed very little, but it had the writhing, squeezing strength of a python. Its legs clenched the professor, and its long, taloned fingers pressed hard, cutting off his air. He feebly tried to beat the brute away, but his hands flopped weakly on its horrible cold slimy sides, and it took no notice of his blows. He tried to grab its wrists, but its skin was as slick as the surface of a slug, and he could get no grip on the thing's arms. "Charley," gasped the professor desperately. "The holy water—"

The creature cut off his wind, and everything began to go dark. The professor rolled on the floor, knocking over the candlesticks, and came to rest with the monster perched on his chest, bending low, opening its grinning mouth to rip out his throat. The professor could see only dimly, through a billowing black fog. He could not get his breath, or even scream. Then he felt moisture, like a shower of rain—and the monster howled!

Dr. Coote crouched on the foot of his bed like the

White Rock girl on her stone. He clutched the holy-water container, and he sprinkled for dear life while he recited the Lord's Prayer in English. The creature let go its hold on the professor's throat and lurched away, trying to shield itself from the deadly spray of water. "Attaboy, Charley!" croaked the professor, crawling away from the monster. "Give it to him! Three cheers and a tiger for the good guys!"

More holy water hit the thing, and with a bawl it suddenly *exploded*. Feathers flew everywhere, a blizzard of pillow stuffing. The professor staggered up, retrieved his glasses, and whooped. A trembling and exhausted Dr. Coote sat back on the bed, his face white. Only then did both men hear the pounding on the door. Professor Childermass had taken the precaution of locking it, and now the nurses were clamoring to get in. The professor rose, brushed stray feathers off himself, and strode to the door. He threw it open to find two wide-eyed nurses staring in. "Yes?" he demanded. "What is the idea of all this noise? This is a hospital, you know, ladies. There are sick people present!"

The nurses gawked at his attire. One red bandanna hung rakishly on his head. More bandannas encircled his stomach. White feathers had settled behind his ears, on top of his head, and on his shoulders. More floated in the air and drifted in heaps across the floor. Behind the professor Dr. Coote was sitting up in bed, trying to figure out how to take the feeding tube out of his nose.

"What—what—what is going *on* here?" the older nurse finally stammered.

Professor Childermass drew himself up. "What does it look like?" he retorted in a crabby voice. "I came to cure my good friend, Dr. Coote, and I have done so. Where your so-called modern medicine failed, I have succeeded. I knew just what he needed all along!"

"What was that?" squawked the dumbfounded nurse.

"A good, old-fashioned, rousing pillow fight!" roared the professor. He reached out and slammed the door right in her face.

Between Dr. Coote's remarkable recovery and Professor Childermass' bellowing insistence, the hospital happily released the patient within the hour. Professor Childermass helped Dr. Coote into the professor's bedraggled old tweed topcoat, because except for his striped pajamas and slippers, Dr. Coote had no clothes of his own at the hospital. The professor helped his old friend downstairs. Dr. Coote was very unsteady on his feet and very light-headed, though for the first time in many weeks he felt his old self. Then the professor drove his Pontiac up to the hospital door and eased Dr. Coote into the passenger seat.

As they roared off for Durham, the professor hastily filled Dr. Coote in on what had been happening. "So," he finished, "we are not out of the woods yet. That hag still has a devil doll in your likeness. My ritual will protect you temporarily, but unless we can find and destroy the doll, she will be able to make you helpless again."

"There is an alternative," said Dr. Coote grimly. "You know, a magician's spells are all broken when he or she dies."

For a moment somber silence filled the car, and then the professor sighed. "It's too bad that neither one of us is a murderer," he said.

Dr. Coote grunted his agreement.

In a few minutes the professor turned the Pontiac in at Dr. Coote's driveway. He got out and went around to help his friend into the house. "That's funny," said Professor Childermass. "Young Lamort should have arrived here by now with the boys, but the house seems to be empty."

"Who?" asked Dr. Coote.

"Todd Lamort," replied the professor tartly. "You remember your own graduate students, don't you?" He put the key in the lock.

"Roderick, I have never had a graduate student named Todd Lamort in my life," said Dr. Coote in a querulous voice.

"You are out of your head," answered the professor. "He is the nicest young man I have met in many a moon—Oh, my God!"

He had opened the door, and both he and Dr. Coote stood transfixed. All the furniture had been taken out of Dr. Coote's living room. Ugly idols and hideous masks hung all over the walls. And on the floor they saw a sinister tracing of red, white, and black lines, making an image like this:

"I know what that is," croaked Dr. Coote in a terrified voice.

"So do I," responded the professor. "It's a *voudon* symbol. Someone has turned your house into a temple of evil!"

Dr. Coote's voice trembled with fear and outrage as he asked, "What fiend would do such a thing?"

Slowly, Professor Childermass put both his hands over his face. "Oh, God forgive me," he moaned. "Charley, I think I have turned Johnny and Byron over to the forces of darkness!" And he began to cry helplessly, uncontrollably, like a man overcome with terrible grief and guilt.

CHAPTER THIRTEEN

"For heaven's sake, Roderick," said Dr. Coote anxiously as the two men stood in the empty, echoing room. "Get a grip on yourself, please! I don't feel very strong, and I've never been good at facing danger, and I have weak legs—"

"D-don't you understand?" wailed Professor Childermass, still weeping wretchedly. "I have g-given those t-two boys to a m-monster! Who knows wh-what he m-may—" He began to sob again.

Dr. Coote grabbed the professor by both shoulders and shook him feebly. It did no good. "Very well," Dr. Coote said at last, his voice dripping with scorn. "Be a big crybaby. I am going to help the boys. You can stay here and snivel—you pompous, swaggering old windbag!"

Professor Childermass' face flamed red at once as outrage boiled in his eyes. "How *dare* you insult me, Charley!" he demanded. "If this is the thanks I get for stuffing your shabby soul back into your miserable Episcopalian carcass, then I wish I'd just let old Slimy Scales take the fool thing. I have *never* been addressed that way in my entire life!" He raised his fists and began to dance around the bare floor like Jack Dempsey, the great heavyweight boxer. "I'll fight you now or later! I'll flatten you like a pin pricking a soap bubble! Get ready to taste canvas, you palooka, you!"

"Good," snorted Dr. Coote, turning his back and hobbling away toward the stairs. "If you are angry, you are at least in the mood to do something. Right now you can help me upstairs so I can get some decent clothes on. Next we'll see about rescuing those boys, and when we've finished that, you can floor me with your haymaker, if you think you can, you old potbellied buzzard!"

Professor Childermass was so angry, he could not speak. He glared at the evil *voudon* design on the floor, and then he began to do a furious tap dance on it, kicking puffs and swathes of colored meal this way and that. He began to rage: "Take *that*! And *that*! You miserable, misbegotten magical markings, I'll snuff you out, one by one!" Then he went tearing around the room, ripping the idols and masks off the walls. He leaped on each one, splintering it to fragments. At last he stood amid the wreckage, panting and grinning ferociously.

Dr. Coote had paused halfway up the stairs and was sitting there, trying to gather strength to go up. He looked on the carnage with wry interest. "Feel better now?" he asked.

"I feel *great*!" roared the professor. "Charley, thanks for shaking me up. I needed that! We may be two old geezers, but by God, we are two *tough* old geezers! Remember the Alamo! Remember the *Maine*!"

"Remember my clothes," said Dr. Coote forlornly. "I am freezing my tail feathers."

Professor Childermass helped Dr. Coote totter upstairs. In a few minutes Dr. Coote was warmly bundled into thick gray flannel trousers, a soft blue flannel shirt, a bulky cable-knit black sweater, and his comfortable old brogans. Then he was hungry, so the professor helped him down to the kitchen. Professor Childermass hesitated for a moment or two before he went to the basement to light the furnace. He remembered too well the horrible zombie that had lurked there. But he gathered his nerve, went downstairs and got the furnace going, and took the time to investigate all the nooks and crannies. There was no zombie.

He returned to the kitchen and rummaged through the larder and refrigerator. He decided that even Todd Lamort, whom he now regarded as a devil incarnate, could not do anything terribly evil to a sealed can of soup. So he heated two cans of Campbell's vegetable beef soup and got two squat brown bottles of Drewry's, Dr. Coote's favorite beer, from the refrigerator. Dr. Coote perked up as he ate, and the professor felt much better after the meal too. "What do we do now?" Dr. Coote asked as he pushed the bowl away from him. "Where will that awful Lamort have taken the boys?"

"Ask me something easy," growled Professor Childermass.

Dr. Coote shook his head. "Really, Roderick, I don't want to be critical, but you should have known better. After all, with a name like Todd Lamort—"

The professor clapped his hand to his head. "Oh, by the hopeful hoplites of Hammurabi!" he bellowed. "*Tod* means 'death' in German, and *la mort* is 'death' in French! How blind a bat can one old fool be? That—that fiend of a graduate student snookered me. If I had him here, I'd—I'd grind his bones to make my bread! I'd—" The professor broke off, his angry expression becoming thoughtful. "Wait a minute!" he shouted. He dragged his wallet out and frantically dug through it, scattering things left and right: A color photograph of his eccentric brother Humphrey, two ticket stubs from a movie he and Johnny had seen a year ago, a 1927 Vermont fishing license—and then he found it. He triumphantly waved a business card. "The biter has been bit! Lamort *gave me his telephone number!*"

Armed with that information, the professor flew into action. He picked up Dr. Coote's phone and dialed the operator. After some bullying and a good deal of coaxing, he scribbled something on a piece of paper. He slammed the receiver down and exulted, "He gave us his phone number, and now the phone company has given us his address!"

"Let's see," said Dr. Coote, holding out his thin hand. He frowned at the writing. "Hmpf. Peculiar—very peculiar. I know roughly where this is, but I can't think of any house on that road. It's near the old ruined Colonial cemetery—oh, of course! There *is* a deserted farmhouse there. It's little more than a tarpaper shack."

"That has to be it," replied the professor. "Mama Sinestra would want to be close to a boneyard to gather her evil forces." He pushed himself away from the table. "Let's go, Charley. Time's a-wastin'."

Dr. Coote wearily shook his head. "Not so fast, Roderick. Settle down, and let's consider this rationally."

"But the boys—"

"The boys," said Dr. Coote in a firm voice, "will be all right as long as we have something that Mama Sinestra and Todd Lamort want. And we do. The drum, in case you have forgotten."

Professor Childermass sank back into his chair. "Heavenly days, McGee! I *had* forgotten the cursed thing."

"Yes," said Dr. Coote. "And if you can manage to listen for a minute, you may learn a thing or two. To begin with, before I fell ill, I discovered some interesting bits of information about *voudon* and especially about the Priests of the Midnight Blood."

"Then tell me," said the professor. "And don't make

me draw it out of you inch by inch, Charley."

Dr. Coote sipped his beer straight from the bottle and told a remarkable and sinister story. The Priests of the Midnight Blood, he said, were a group of *voudon* sorcerers led by none other than Corinne LeGrande, better known as Mama Sinestra. Their symbol was a red drop of blood in a circle, with a white teardrop-shaped highlight in the blood drop. The two superimposed shapes resembled the hands of a clock pointing straight up—a reference to the name of the group, the Midnight Blood priesthood.

These people had gained their wicked reputation on the island of St. Ives and their diabolic name by sacrificing one human life a day, for a whole year, to the powers of darkness. Three hundred sixty-five times they had slit the throats of their poor victims. Midnight after midnight they had spilled the innocent blood of men, women, and children to attract and gain control over demonic forces. And they had used their dark magic for many years to keep the LeGrande family on the throne. Because the Priests of the Midnight Blood dealt with deadly forces, they were the leaders of the Cult of the Baron. Baron Samedi, the Lord of the Dead, could be summoned by the beating of drums, and he granted the abominable wishes of the priesthood. Under his rule zombies walked by night, snuffing out the lives of all who opposed the harsh rule of General LeGrande.

However, a small resistance movement had begun after World War II, and Dr. Coote said that the young man who had given him the drum was no doubt a member of that resistance. "The very morning I fell so dreadfully ill," Dr. Coote explained, "I had a phone call from the New Orleans police. They had discovered the body of a man who fit the description of the unfortunate young fellow who passed the drum along to me. He had a program from the academic conference in his pocket and he had circled my name. The police say his body was—well, he had been savagely killed. And they discovered his name was François Devereaux, and he was, until recently, the valet to General Hippolyte LeGrande, of St. Ives."

"I see," said Professor Childermass slowly. "This poor man absconded with the drum, and without the drum the priests could no longer do their dirty work. That is why the revolution in St. Ives against General LeGrande has almost succeeded."

"Has it?" asked Dr. Coote, a dark satisfaction in his voice. "Good! But I also figured out why the drum was so important. Young Devereaux had taken it just before a big ceremony, while the *loa*, or spirit, of the Baron of the Dead was in the drum. By the way, you told me you wondered why the vandals who ransacked my house didn't break anything. It was for a very good reason: They were afraid I had transferred this spirit into some object inside my house, and if they happened to break whatever housed the *loa*, then the entity would burst forth in all his uncontrolled power. By accident Fergie let just a little of that power out by beating the drum, and the result rocked your house to the foundation. Imagine what it could do if it burst out at full force—or if a genuine *voudon* priestess pounded out her unholy rhythm on that prehistoric drumhead!"

Professor Childermass felt a chill, although the house was growing warmer by the minute. "Prehistoric?"

With a bleak smile, Dr. Coote said, "I'll tell you more about that some other time. But the important thing is, I learned how to make the spirit in the drum absolutely helpless. You see, the *loas* have no power if they are in a river. Running water insulates them, turns them in on their evil selves."

"You chunked it in the river?" asked the professor.

"Not quite." Dr. Coote rose. "Come with me."

They went to Dr. Coote's bedroom, and then into the bathroom. His toilet was the old-fashioned kind with a tank high on the wall and a lever with a chain attached that you had to pull to flush. At Dr. Coote's urging, the professor dragged a chair into the bathroom and climbed up on it. He took off the top of the toilet tank and thrust his arm inside, grimacing at the cold water. He hauled out something sealed in a waterproof oilcloth bag, something the size and shape of a large Dixie cup. "No wonder the blasted toilet wouldn't stop dribbling," muttered the professor, stepping down.

"Of course it wouldn't," growled Dr. Coote. "I used a nail to stick a hole in the flush ball. The water has to be *running*, remember."

Professor Childermass groaned. "And idiot that I am, I let Lamort stay here! It's lucky for us he never investigated this drippy tank himself."

"It certainly is," responded Dr. Coote dryly. "On the other hand, he probably never even thought of the tank as the equivalent of a running river. After all, the drum is something that he would revere, and one doesn't think of revered objects in such unlikely places."

The professor stood with the oilcloth package dripping in his hands. "Well, now that we have this, any suggestions? We have to save the boys, but I have a sneaky suspicion that if we turn this over to dear sweet Mama S., we're all gone gooses anyway."

"Geese," muttered Dr. Coote, who hated to hear words misused. "We have to reach a bargain somehow, and make it so binding that not even the evil Priests of the Midnight Blood can break their word. Shall we go to see Todd Lamort now?"

Just then the telephone rang. Professor Childermass narrowed his eyes. "No one knows we're here," he said. "But I'll bet you my own phalanges against the five chunks of bone on this drum that the person calling us right now is either Todd Lamort—or Mama Sinestra!"

CHAPTER FOURTEEN

Johnny struggled to loosen the rope that tied his hands behind him. Beside him on the backseat of the cold, rusty old Ford, Fergie was writhing too. Night had fallen. Todd Lamort drove his rickety car, and in the front passenger seat sat his grandmother, the evil Mama Sinestra. All that day Johnny and Fergie had been locked in a chilly, windowless room of the ramshackle old farmhouse. They had tried to think of a way of escape, but none had come to them. Fergie discovered, however, that he could press his head against one of the walls and hear their captors talking on the other side. That was how the boys knew what lay before them tonight.

Fergie had heard Lamort's side of a telephone conversation with Professor Childermass. From the sound of it, the boys' captors were bargaining for something that they wanted in exchange for Johnny and Fergie. They wanted the professor to bring the drum to the farmhouse, but the old man must have balked at that idea. Finally, Lamort agreed to meet Professor Childermass somewhere else. After the phone conversation was over, Fergie heard some chilling words. First, Lamort laughed in a nasty way. "The old fool chose the place where you found your servant. What an idiot he is! He really thinks we will make the exchange and then let him and those two brats go free," he had said.

And with an ugly laugh of her own, his grandmother answered, "Then he is worse than a fool. I think perhaps tonight we will gain more good servants, eh, my grandson?"

"High time that we killed our enemies. I would never have handled things the way you did," returned Lamort, sounding whiny and petulant. "You sent that old fool into a coma, and then you made me sit by his side day after day, just in case he talked. I would have used the power of magic to *force* him to talk."

The old woman fairly snarled: "You ambitious young fool! We are in a strange place, and our powers are not at their strongest here. What good would it do to torture the old man if torture would kill him? Then where would we be? All those weeks you stayed in his house or at his bedside, and you never even came close to finding out where he hid the drum."

"But when I get to be a priest—"

"Silence!" snapped the old woman.

And that was all Fergie could hear. "Whaddaya suppose the old bat meant by *good servants?*" asked Fergie.

"I think she wants to—to turn us into zombies," gulped Johnny.

Fergie looked very angry at that. "Just let the old battleaxe try!" he growled.

That had been not long after noon. Since then, Lamort had driven away from the house, had stayed away for several hours, and had returned. At twilight he and Mama Sinestra came to tie the boys up and herd them into the icy old Ford. Hungry, frightened, and half frozen, they jounced along as Lamort drove to the meeting place. Johnny and Fergie were low in the seat, and although he could not see much, Johnny got the idea that they were heading back toward Portsmouth.

"Where ya takin' us?" demanded Fergie.

"Shut up," ordered Lamort, who was still in a mean, surly mood. "*Grand-mère*, we soon will be going through the town. Make sure these brats don't cry out."

The old crone twisted around in her seat. She made some mystic signs in the air and chanted:

"Magic law, lockjaw! Silence now rules!
Freeze lungs, hold tongues, quiet these fools!"

Fergie made an odd choking sound, and Johnny felt his tongue and jaw turn very cold, as if he had closed his mouth on a round ball of ice. He struggled to talk but couldn't. He panicked, because he had always been terrified of stepping on a rusty nail and getting tetanus, or lockjaw, and now he thought the voodoo witch had somehow given him the disease. He struggled desperately but managed only a soft squeak or two.

"You should have done better than that," complained Lamort. "I still hear them."

"The fair one is fighting the spell," answered the old woman. She gave an evil chuckle. "Let him struggle! The more he fights, the stronger the magic will grow!"

That at last made Johnny try to relax. When he did, the terrible vise that clamped his mouth shut and the invisible band that tightened on his chest both eased. He realized that the spell merely kept him from crying out or screaming a warning. If he breathed slowly and regularly, he thought he might be able to whisper, so he tried to save his strength.

At last the car stopped, but the night was so dark that Johnny could not see where they were. "We are early," Lamort said. "I'll just get things ready for our little meeting." He climbed out of the car. Johnny heard him go around back and unlock the trunk, but he did not seem to take anything out of it. In a moment Lamort had climbed back into the driver's seat. "It won't be long," he said. "Did you bring the doll?"

"I have it here," Mama Sinestra said. "Tonight, if you like, we will use it to kill the old man. He was the beginning of all our troubles."

"No, *Grand-mère*," Lamort said. "I gave my word that we would turn over the boys and the doll if the dear professor will give us what we want." He giggled. "Of course, I said nothing about what might happen *after* we make the exchange, so if you should find the doll of Dr. Coote lying around on the ground then, why, I wouldn't object if you wanted to stab a pin or two through the heart."

Both of them laughed. Johnny's heart sank. He knew all too well that these wicked people had no intention of letting him, Fergie, the professor, or Dr. Coote live. His mind raced furiously. How could he warn the professor about what the two were plotting to do?

After a few minutes Mama Sinestra muttered, "Eh, I will be glad to return once more to St. Ives, where it is warm all the year. This cold hurts my old bones."

"We will be home again soon enough," responded La-mort. "And when we are, we will use your magic to kill all those foolish rebels who thought they could overthrow Papa. Then you will teach me to wield the power of the drum and be a Priest of the Midnight Blood, just like Papa."

The old woman's voice was firm and angry as she said, "Not until you are ready, my grandson."

Lamort burst into belligerence: "Curse you, I am ready now! I have served you for seven years already. I want to use my powers to punish those fools who have insulted and blocked me. The magic should be strong in me by now."

The old woman snarled, "Foolish boy!"

"How am I foolish?" he demanded. "Didn't I take care

of these two meddlers? Didn't I keep watch on the old man in the hospital?"

"Didn't you tell all sorts of idiotic lies?" taunted Mama Sinestra. "Saying you were a student, you had organized a blood drive—how easily our enemies could have checked any of those imbecilic stories! You had the luck of a fool, no?"

"No one *did* check," argued Lamort stubbornly. "And I am sure that I am ready to be a priest, that I could summon a spirit just as you do."

The old woman snorted. "Anyone can summon a spirit with the drum—but can you control it? I think not, my grandson. And if you summoned a spirit without being able to direct it, it would be better for you had you never been born."

After a moment Lamort said sullenly, "If *I* controlled the drum, I would turn them all into zombies! Such peasants deserve to be punished even beyond death. And when we are the masters again, we will—"

"Shh," said Mama Sinestra. "There is a light."

"It must be the professor," muttered Lamort. "All right! Everyone out!"

He got out of the car and pulled the back door open. Johnny's and Fergie's ankles were not tied, so they could stand. It took Johnny a moment to get his bearings. The car was parked on a slushy street, but no lights showed anywhere. Then a glow came from ahead. Johnny recognized the glare of headlights, and he saw silhouetted shapes. His heart thudded. They were in another cemetery, with rows and rows of headstones all around them. A nearby grave was thick with wreaths, as if the funeral had been that very day. What had Lamort said about the place where Mama Sinestra had found her first servant? Of course—this must be the graveyard where poor Mr. Dupont had been buried! Why had the professor agreed to meet the evil sorceress and her grandson in such a place?

"Wait here," ordered Lamort as he reached in through the driver's window and turned on the Ford's headlights. They glowed a sickly yellow and showed the snow-covered hills of the cemetery. Johnny edged slowly away from the car, and silently Fergie followed him. They did not go a great distance—just a few feet. Still, they moved to a place where they could back up against a tall, spiky monument. Johnny stretched his wrists as far apart as he could and began to rub the rope binding them against the rough stone. He could hear Fergie doing the same thing. *Just keep Mama Sinestra away for a couple of minutes*, he thought, *and we can get free.*

And then what? Johnny had no idea—he just knew that he wanted desperately to get out of his bonds and to run from the despicable old woman and her treacherous grandson. Where was she, anyway? Mama Sinestra had melted into the darkness, and Johnny could not tell where she might be lurking.

The approaching car stopped about fifty feet away. Johnny heard doors slam, and then he saw a short figure and a tall, weedy one step into the space between the cars. His heart leaped. Although he had to lean on a cane, Dr. Coote was up and walking, and Professor Childermass was at his side. Then Johnny remembered the deadly trap that the two were walking into, and he felt a wrenching stab of despair. He heard his elderly friend's raspy, cantankerous voice: "All right, blast you, Lamort, here's your package. Turn over the boys and the doll, and you can have it."

"Gladly," said Lamort. He turned back and said, "Come on, boys. Your gallant rescuers are here!"

Johnny gave one last desperate rub, but he did not break through the rope. He and Fergie stumbled forward. Lamort held something up. "I will put the doll in the blond boy's jacket," he said. He unzipped Johnny's jacket and stuck the voodoo doll inside. In the light from the two cars, Johnny was able to glimpse it. The doll might have been featureless when first made, but now it was a little replica of Dr. Coote, down to the fluffy hair on the crown of his head and the horn-rimmed spectacles. "All right," said Lamort, "the boys will walk forward. You come to meet them, Professor. Place the drum on the road when you get to them. Then back up with them, but no more than ten feet. When I have the drum and have returned to my car, you may leave."

Johnny heard Fergie straining, but all his friend could do was make desperate little *mmph!* noises. The freezing enchantment was still holding Johnny's tongue too, though he desperately wanted to shout a warning.

"Very well," said Professor Childermass. "Here I come."

"Boys," said Lamort, "go join your friends, but walk slowly."

Johnny and Fergie walked almost in step through the slushed snow as the professor came forward to meet them. He had a bundle under his arm. When they were very close, Lamort cried out, "Stop! I want to see the drum!"

The professor held the bundle up. It was wrapped in oilcloth. Dramatically, he unwrapped it. The hateful little drum was inside, its ebony-colored body gleaming dully in the glare of the car headlights. "There," said Professor Childermass. "Is that what you want, you snake in the grass?"

"That is it," said Lamort. "Put down the drum, and then back away with the boys. I am coming to get our property."

The professor carefully rewrapped the drum and set it down. "Come along, gentlemen," he said. "We're almost out of this."

Johnny and Fergie went to join him. They backed away. Lamort came cautiously forward, picked up the drum, and retreated toward his car, unwrapping the package. He laughed in a wild, triumphant way when he held the drum in his hands. "You fools!" he shouted. "Now, *Grand-mère*! Release the zombie!"

Behind Johnny Dr. Coote cried out in alarm. Professor

Childermass seized Johnny's and Fergie's shoulders and spun them around so they could run for the safety of his Pontiac. Too late! A plodding, shambling figure had broken into the light from behind Dr. Coote. It stalked toward them, cutting off their escape.

Johnny strained again at his bonds—and they snapped! He must have worn the rope almost completely through against the granite monument. With a careless swipe of its arms the zombie shoved Professor Childermass aside, and he went tumbling down. Fergie staggered away from the creature, but lost his footing and fell to his knees. Somewhere to the left a pipe played a weird tune, and the zombie's head swung blindly toward the struggling boy. The figure stooped and seized Fergie and swung him up over his shoulder like a sack of potatoes. Then the zombie blundered toward Johnny.

Johnny ran, his heart exploding with terror. So that was what Mama Sinestra meant—she and Lamort would kill Dr. Coote and the professor and make zombies out of him and Fergie! Lamort stepped to intercept him, but Johnny swerved around beside the Ford. He slipped and fell, and his hands sloshed through the slushy snow as he tried to catch himself. The rope burns on his wrists suddenly stung as though he had rubbed alcohol into them. Alcohol or—salt!

Salt was the one thing that could break the spell animating a zombie! What had the professor said? In New Hampshire, they threw salt all over the roads! The fresh grave meant that the cemetery drive had been sprinkled with rock salt. Johnny grabbed a double handful of slush and spun. The zombie was almost on top of him. He would have only one chance. Desperately, he threw the slushy snowball as hard as he could.

Splat! It connected. The slush splashed across the zombie's face. It dripped from the creature's cheekbones and chin and nose. And it must have dribbled into its open mouth.

The figure stopped. Fergie kicked himself loose and fell to the ground with a *whump*. As Johnny watched fearfully, the zombie's black, dead tongue came out and licked its black, dead lips. Then the blank eyes smoldered with awareness. Awareness and hatred. The zombie turned and lurched away into the darkness. "Where are you going?" shouted Lamort. "*Grand-mère*, what is wrong?"

The pipes played frantically. The zombie growled, a harsh, awful, inhuman sound. From ahead of it in the dark came the terrified screams of Mama Sinestra: "No! No! Keep away, I command you! Help me! Help me! Not into the grave, I order you! No! My grandson, help me! *Helllp meee. . . .*"

The screech faded to an awful wail, and then silence. Johnny staggered and gasped as an invisible fist loosened its hold on him. His frozen mouth suddenly felt hot, as if he had taken a gulp of scalding tea. "I can talk!" he said.

"Joy of joys," growled the sopping-wet Fergie, who had staggered to his knees. "Help me up, Dixon, and get these ropes off me!"

It had all taken just a moment. Professor Childermass had risen too, and he was stalking toward Lamort, with Dr. Coote close behind him, brandishing his cane like a club. "Now," thundered the professor, "by heaven, sir, defend yourself! I'll teach you to play such a shabby trick—"

His eyes wild, Lamort thumped the drum in a broken rhythm. "I summon thee, Lord of the Dead!" he cried. "Come and help thy servant!"

Johnny blinked as the air in front of Lamort grew dark and solid. A terrible figure shimmered there. A figure with a skull face and a top hat and a shabby, torn frock coat. Baron Samedi himself had come to answer the drumbeat!

But something was dreadfully wrong. Slowly, the immense form turned to face the man who held the black drum. Slowly, he reached out a skeletal hand for Lamort. The young man screamed in terror as the bony fingers entered his chest. Johnny groaned, but he could not tear his eyes away from the grisly scene. He saw no wound, no blood—the ghostly fingers of the Baron had passed right through Lamort's body as if it were made of mist or water! Then Lamort reeled as the living skeleton's hand came out again, clenched into a fist. Something glowing golden-yellow, something like a huge frantic moth, struggled and fluttered in that clenched cage of bone—and then the fingers crunched shut, and the light died. Lamort dropped the drum and fell in a heap, babbling senselessly. The enormous skeleton reared to its full height and slowly vanished, fading into the darkness of the night.

"What—what happened?" gasped Fergie.

Dr. Coote came slowly up, leaning on his cane. "He was not an initiated priest," murmured the old man, looking down at Lamort with a strange sort of pity. "The Lord of the Dead turned against him and plucked his soul right out of his body. This miserable wretch will be what he tried to make of you: a mindless, helpless, soulless zombie!"

CHAPTER FIFTEEN

"Gee, Doc, what were you gonna do if Dixon hadn't been such a good shot with a snowball?" asked Fergie.

It was New Year's Eve, and once again Professor Childermass was having a little party. Father Higgins, Dr. Coote, Fergie, and Johnny were his guests, and Fergie was full of questions. The day after they had returned to Duston Heights from New Hampshire, Fergie's parents had taken him to Ohio to spend Christmas with his grandmother. He had returned only this afternoon, and he wanted to know all about what had happened in his absence.

"Well," murmured Dr. Coote, carefully sipping his brandy, "Roderick and I had a few tricks up our sleeves.

I had memorized some protective magic spells that *might* work against evil magic, and Roderick had—well, to be blunt, he had a weapon. You see, Fergie, we suspected the zombie would show up, and like you and Johnny, we knew how to deal with it. So Roderick packed a gun."

"That's right," said the professor with a fierce grin. "As a matter of fact, I suggested that cemetery precisely because I wanted to fire my weapon in the place where it would do the most good. Too bad I didn't have a chance to discharge it. It was a nifty little Flash Gordon squirt pistol loaded with salt water! I intended to spritz that undead monstrosity right in the mush, but John Michael beat me to it!"

They all laughed. It was past ten o'clock. Fergie's mom and dad and Johnny's grandparents thought the celebration was just to see the New Year in, but the friends had other matters to discuss as well. On the hearth was the black drum, and they had to decide what to do with it.

"What happened to Mama Sinestra?" asked Fergie.

"Ah," said Dr. Coote. "Well, Roderick arranged to meet Lamort and the, ah, lady, in the same part of the cemetery where Mr. Dupont had been buried before they turned him into a zombie. When Johnny broke the spell and the zombie regained his memory, he sank back into the earth and returned to his grave. I am afraid he took Mrs. LeGrande along. You see, a zombie who recovered his human understanding would not feel very kindly toward those who had created the evil enchantment."

"Remember how we could suddenly talk again?" Johnny asked Fergie. "That was when the zombie pulled her down into the grave."

Fergie shuddered. "So what about the super-duper magical whammy pincushion doll?"

Father Higgins nodded toward a brown paper bag that lay on the hearth before the fire. "Take a look for yourself," he said. "Johnny says that when he looked inside his jacket, where Lamort had put the doll, that was all he could find."

Curiously, Fergie emptied the bag. It held nothing but some pinkish cloth, some white cloth, some dirty-yellow cotton batting, and a few white hairs. "I get it," Fergie said. "When ol' Mama S. croaked, all her spells went bye-bye."

"Speaking of going bye-bye," said Professor Childermass, "you might be interested in a few more tidbits of news. First, the man who called himself Todd Lamort was really Etienne LeGrande, the youngest son of General LeGrande, the former dictator of St. Ives."

"Former dictator?" asked Johnny.

The professor nodded solemnly. "According to *The New York Times*, his oppressive government fell the very night that we defeated Mama Sinestra. He is imprisoned on the island now, waiting trial under the new democracy that the rebels are setting up. As for his son—well, we arranged for him to be checked into a charity mental hospital as 'John Doe,' an unknown. He is totally helpless. He cannot talk sense, feed himself, or understand what anyone says. He is a zombie—only no spirit lives in his empty mind. I am afraid he will remain like that for the rest of his wretched life."

Johnny knew that he himself had barely escaped Lamort's horrible fate. "Now we have one thing left to do," he told Fergie. "We have to destroy the drum."

Dr. Coote grimaced. "I hate to do it, in a way," he admitted. "It is a rare, even a unique object, and there may be nothing like that drumhead in the world. You see, St. Ives is a volcanic island, and when settlers first came to it, they reported some odd creatures they called 'devil birds' that nested in the caldera of the old volcano. They were supposed to be like huge birds, but hairless, with wings like those of bats. The settlers gradually killed them all, but the drumhead is made of the skin that was stretched tight over the wings of such a creature."

Johnny blinked. "Hairless birds with wings like those of bats? That sounds like a pterodactyl," he said.

"Wow!" said Fergie. "The Lost World! Modern-day dinosaurs living in a Caribbean hideaway! D'you hafta destroy it, Doc?"

"We've talked it over," said Father Higgins. "We all agree that it must be done."

So late that night everyone trooped out into the professor's backyard, where he built a fire in the incinerator. As it was beginning to crackle, Fergie coughed and said, "Dixon, there's one more thing I gotta know. You were supposed t' tell your dad if you wanted t' move away or stay here. What did you decide?"

Johnny hesitated. "Well," he said at last, "I know how much Dad loves the Air Force. And I know that I'd miss Father Higgins, and Dr. Coote, and Gramma and Grampa, and the professor. Still, he's my dad, and I was going to tell him I wanted to move away and live with him."

Fergie took a deep breath. In a strained voice he muttered, "Aw, Dixon. I guess I understand—"

"Hang on," said Johnny. "I just said I *was* going to tell him that I'd live with him. But then I started wondering who'd be around to save you from the next monster, Fergie, so I told him I'd decided to stay with Gramma and Grampa."

Fergie whooped and gave Johnny a playful sock on the arm. The two pushed each other around, laughing like loons, until Professor Childermass coughed and said, "Now, gentlemen, contain yourselves—though I have to admit that I myself am pleased that John will stick around here in dull, boring old Duston Heights, where nothing exciting ever happens!"

Then the fire roared up, and Dr. Coote muttered, "Here goes nothing." He gingerly tossed the drum onto the blaze as Father Higgins pronounced a solemn prayer of blessing. Orange flames licked the black sides of the drum. The hideous image of Baron Samedi charred and blackened. The thongs snapped, the bones crackled, and the leather drumhead shriveled in the heat. Then the wood burst into fire, glowing a brilliant yellow. Suddenly, with a great *whoosh*, a ball of reddish-orange flame shot straight up, like a rocket. Everyone gasped and stepped back. Johnny blinked. Was it his imagination, or did the ball of flame take on a shape? It seemed to him that great bat wings spread out, and a dragonlike head writhed at the end of a long, snaky neck. Then the wings beat once, twice, three times, and the flame creature sped away to the south, fading as it flew.

Just then all the bells in Duston Heights began to ring out. "Great heavens!" said the professor, clapping his mittened hands over his ears. "Now we've done it! Did everyone in town see that monster flying through the sky?"

Fergie laughed. "Aw, Prof," he said, "we're not as important as all that! It's just midnight, that's all. Happy New Year!"

They all laughed and wished each other a happy New Year. Johnny looked up at the midnight sky. The fiery flying thing had vanished, and a million twinkling stars glittered against the black-velvet heavens like so many brilliant diamonds. Johnny took a deep breath of the sweet, cold air of Duston Heights and felt himself at home and at peace with the world.